BAD DECISIONS MAKE GOOD STORIES

CHARLIE MCOUAT

BAD DECISIONS MAKE GOOD STORIES

iUniverse books may be ordered through booksellers or by contacting:

iUniverse
1663 Liberty Drive
Bloomington, IN 47403
www.iuniverse.com
1-800-Authors (1-800-288-4677)

Because of the dynamic nature of the Internet, any web addresses or links contained in this book may have changed since publication and may no longer be valid. The views expressed in this work are solely those of the author and do not necessarily reflect the views of the publisher, and the publisher hereby disclaims any responsibility for them.

Any people depicted in stock imagery provided by Getty Images are models, and such images are being used for illustrative purposes only. Certain stock imagery © Getty Images.

ISBN: 978-1-5320-4765-7 (sc)
ISBN: 978-1-5320-4766-4 (e)

Library of Congress Control Number: 2018904470

Print information available on the last page.

iUniverse rev. date: 04/17/2018

Contents

GOOD STORIES

1

Bad Decisions Make Good Stories

Lorrie and I are lucky. We seem to have enough money to last until the Grim Reaper pays a visit but who knows? Our financial security is aided by our reluctance to spend money. Sometimes we tease each other about our irrational frugality.

We celebrated this holiday season by taking the cheapest, not best, cruise line we could find, Holland America. We had traveled with them once before so thought we knew every way to save a dollar. I emptied a forty-eight-ounce bottle of Listerine mouthwash so I could fill it with food colored vodka to drink instead of paying bar side prices. On a two-week Caribbean Cruise that would save us at least $28.50. Of course, we'd have to imbibe in our crowded room instead of a bar room with an ocean view. We reserved the cheapest room with an "obstructed view."

Our "obstructed view," was "no view," unless you consider a lifeboat obliterating the ocean as a view. We saved another $15 by parking at the Park Doctor. The "Parktologist," as he called himself, was miles away from the port but another chance to save a few pennies. Our ship offered their own tour of Mahogany Bay in Honduras for $40 apiece.

"No way," I said, "We can do a lot better than that. We'll walk off the ship and hire someone local."

"Yes, but the cruise line warns against that. If anything happens they are not responsible. Maybe we ought to just pay the $40." I hate it when she's so logical.

"No way am I going to pay that outrageous fee. There'll be plenty of Hondurans anxious to show us around."

We walked off the Oosterdam, past the lines of people waiting for their air conditioned, luxurious, tour of Mahogany Bay. I felt sorry for those poor suckers paying full price. Within a quarter of a mile, we approached a tent with a prominent sign welcoming us, "Tour Mahogany Bay." I was so proud of myself. "Lorrie, this is it. See how easy it is?"

A beautiful black woman with bright Caribbean dress smiled at me. I melted. "Would you like a tour of our beautiful island, Sir?"

I thought, "This place is so friendly."

She said, "We have fully certified, experienced guides ready to show you around this Caribbean paradise." I looked behind me at a line of modern vans. Lorrie asked, "Do they speak English?" I thought that was a silly question after she just told us they are 'certified.'

"Oh certainly. They are all fully certified."

"How much?" I asked.

"Thirty-five dollars."

"For both?"

"Oh no sir. Thirty-five apiece for our best guide."

"See Lorrie, that will save us $10," I said like I had just closed a major business deal. "Will you take a credit card?" Sometimes I can be a bit naive.

"No. Cash only."

"Are you sure he can speak English?" Lorrie repeated. Sometimes her negativity can be annoying. I held her hand to reassure her as the lady spoke in Spanish over her cell phone. I studied Spanish fifty years ago in college so was surprised that I couldn't understand a word of her conversation. I assumed that it was due to my hearing loss.

Lorrie's worry lines were becoming more prominent. I paid the seventy dollars. Clouds were darkening the sky. After ten minutes of fidgeting together, a rusted-out Ford Escort pulled in behind the vans in front of the tent office. A smiling Honduran hoped out, extended his hand, "Hello, mi name is Marlin. Welcome. I be your guide today." He spoke slowly, deliberately like an elementary school actor trying to recite lines in his first play.

He opened the door and extended his hand to help Lorrie into the back seat. I tried to follow but he closed the door and motioned for me to sit up front with him. "This is a macho country," I chuckled. "Men first." I fumbled with the seat belt but it wouldn't snap shut. "I do," he said.

After another two minutes of poking and prying I heard it "Snap."

He pulled away from the parking lot and I thought I'd test my college Spanish. "Your isla es bonita."

His face lit up, "Oh, you speak Spanish?"

"Un Poco," this was going to be fun, impressing a native with my long-lost language skill.

From the back-seat Lorrie said, "Charlie, speak English. This trip is not for you to practice your Spanish." Sometimes I don't hear my wonderful wife when she speaks.

It started raining, a few drops at first and then a downpour. We couldn't see out the windows. He switched on the wipers and his side immediately flew off.

"Rain," he said.

"Si lluvia. Mucho rain." I was relieved when he stopped the car because I was sure he couldn't see a thing out of his wiperless windshield. He walked in front, retrieved the errant wiper and coaxed it back into its proper place. We could see again and proceeded.

The semi paved road was loaded with car swallowing pot holes and frequent speed bumps. I asked myself, "Why would they bother with speed bumps when the pot holes prevent anything more than a cautious crawl."

We went over a bridge.

"Bridge," he said.

We passed an orchard, "Banana," as he pointed at a tree. He was showing off his English vocabulary.

"Dog," he pointed towards an emaciated pooch.

Because of his non-English, Lorrie felt safe in wisecracking from behind, "Charlie, what are we going to do with that ten dollars we saved by taking this bargain tour? Invest it?" Sarcasm is not one of her attractions.

A road sign read, "Calle peligroso."

I turned to Marlin, "This road is very dangerous." No response. I tried again, "Este calle muy peligroso."

"No Problema," he shrugged.

I tried to continue our conversation without Lorrie freaking out in the back seat.

"Marlin, countos tiempos since un accidente?"

"Yo no tiene accidente por dos semanas."

Lorrie comes alive, "Charlie, I know 'accidente' is 'accident.' 'What is semanas?"

"Semanas is years," I lied.

"No señor, 'semanas' es 'weeks' no 'years,'" Marlin corrected my intentional error in translation.

Lorrie yelled, "Charlie, I know when you're fibbing. Marlin had an accident two weeks ago, not years ago."

In twenty-four years of marriage I have not fooled her one time. "Charlie, either let me out right here, right now or turn this car around. It's pouring, this car's about to fall apart, he speaks no English. Let them keep the $70. I want to go back to the ship, now."

Marlin is puzzled by her hysteria. "Senor, que pasa?"

I try to explain, "Marlin, mi expose (wife) quiere (wants) to "return" (don't know the Spanish for 'return') el barco (ship)."

Somehow, he understands my feeble attempt at his language. He turns the car, "Tal vez mañana? No hoy."

"Yes Marlin, maybe tomorrow, not today."

2

Biakpa and the Eagle

Biakpa is a small village in the Volta Region of Ghana. From anywhere in town you can look up and see the highest mountain in West Africa. Lush vegetation, tall trees and shrubs obscure a dirt road meandering up the mountainside, leading to another isolated village at the peak. It is quiet here. Occasionally a hawk circles above or a dove coos in the distance, but most wild game has been hunted and devoured for food.

Few people In Biakpa have electricity and those that do, use it sparingly. The nearby Volta River was dammed up years ago to produce electricity for the whole country but constant drought has dried up the source and weakened the power. Rationing, two days off, one day on, is accepted throughout the country. Electricity is a luxury, a new toy for the few people lucky enough to be supplied.

In town, a road of hard packed sand and clay, with loose stones big enough to puncture the bottom of any car, winds through the center of Biakpa. Deep ruts, eroded banking, and children playing dictate that the rare car passing through, proceed with caution.

People live in cement block huts with straw roofs and floors of either clay or a cement. Residents spend a lot of time outdoors cleaning their entrance ways, cooking food, or socializing with neighbors. Money is seldom used. In the town center, a huge Boaboa tree marks the village meeting place where men gather to discuss their lives as they've done for centuries. A few paces beyond, women congregate to pump water from the village well. They stand straight, with their heads steady to balance buckets filled with water, food, or goods to trade with neighbors. Farmers trade their fruit for someone else's vegetables and everybody shares.

I look down an embankment and watch women wade in a shallow stream scrubbing their family's clothes, lining the banks with spotless shirts, pants, and dresses spreading them to dry in the equatorial sun. This is another place for gossip and female bonding.

A large, newly constructed African Methodist Church sits high on solid rock offering the main Christian alternative to traditional African religions. A staircase, like a stairway to heaven, leads the parishioners into

6

the narthex. The white walls seem to spring from the Earth, majestic, offering sanctuary from the stress of everyday life and a daily reminder of where to find solace.

The road continues on, curving past huts on each side, then ascends towards the edge of town. To the right, a wide pathway leads up a steep well-trodden path to the school. A wooden sign, reading, "Biakpa Forms One, Two. And Three," beckons the children to learn to read and write. The wooden sign is not yet aged, like the school, showing that formal education is a new phenomenon in the area. The school is a long, cylindrical cement block building consisting of three rooms, one for each grade level. A huge, brightly painted map of Ghana, bisects the outside wall, giving visitors a patriotic greeting. The villagers are proud of their families, their country, and now, their school

I had volunteered to teach in this idyllic little town and was now facing my first day of class. I assumed that I would start off as a teaching assistant and gradually work into my own class. Instead, I arrived at school at eight o'clock on that first morning and was directed into a room full of eager students. A Peace Corps volunteer introduced me as their new teacher and promptly left the room. I forced a smile and faced about forty young Ghanaians, crowded together on backless benches, staring up at the old guy with the colorless skin who would be their teacher for the next month. I didn't know if they could speak English, what their learning level was, or if they could read or write. They appeared to vary in age between ten and sixteen years old.

The cement block room was opened on two sides to let in the sunshine. There was no electricity, books, or teaching aids. A blackboard covered the front of the room. I smiled, they smiled as they leaned forward win their benches, anxious for me to begin. I thought, *"Charlie, are you up to this? What are you doing here? You're out of your league. This is not your world."*

I took a deep breath, picked up a tiny fragment of chalk and wrote my name on the blackboard. I wrote, "C-H-A-R-L-I-E M-C-O-U-A-T," sounding out each letter. They echoed my words and giggled at the way I pronounced the letters. They seemed to understand me so I told them about my country, The United States of America. I wrote each sentence, turning the sound of my voice into written words on the blackboard. I felt that we understood each other through the miracle of sounds, writing, talking, and listening.

I asked, "When the United States played Ghana in the World cup, who won?"

They laughed, clapped, and shouted in unison, "Ghana. Ghana. Ghana won. We won."

We laughed together and I add, "When Ghana beat the United States, I'm sure the whole world was happy, including me." I'm now on a roll, having fun, glad to be in their country, and bonding with these beautiful people.

I invite each of them to come to the board, write their name and tell me if they have brothers and sisters

Ghana was colonized by the British so their national language is English but they speak in local languages, mostly Ga. Biakpa is about six hours of treacherous travel from the capital city of Accra. I asked, "Have any of you been to Accra?" No one raised their hand. No one had ventured that far from Biakpa.

With about an hour to go before the end of class, four official looking town elders entered the room, nodded to me, then stood silently against the back wall. I'm sure they were there to check if the stranger could be trusted with their precious children. While I was wondering what this ex-dentist, non-teacher was going to do, a story came to mind. I said, "I'm going to tell this story very slowly and each of you take turns coming to the blackboard and writing it down as I recite. Then we'll read it together and discuss it. I began:

"Once there was a baby eagle who got separated from his momma. A farmer rescued the eagle and put it in the barnyard with his chickens. The baby eagle learned to live like a chicken. He groveled in the dirt for food, worms, grubs, and bugs like a chicken. One day a man visited the farm, saw the eagle acting like a chicken. He carried him to the top of a stepladder and said, 'You are an eagle, not a chicken. Now fly eagle, fly.' The eagle got scared. He was comfortable in the dirt with the chickens. He flapped his wings a few times, gave up and fell back into the dust of the barnyard.

A few months later, another man came, saw the eagle, and took him to the roof of the barn. He held the eagle out at arm's length and said, 'You are an eagle not a chicken. Now fly eagle fly.' The eagle was scared. He flapped his wings a few times, gave up and fell back where he was comfortable, in the barnyard with the chickens.

A while later another man saw the eagle pecking in the dirt. He grabbed the eagle and took him to the highest mountain in the area. He held out the eagle and said, "You are an eagle not a chicken. You belong up here high in the sky. Now fly eagle fly.' The eagle was scared, but this time he went into himself and said, 'I am an eagle. I am. I can fly.' He flapped his wings, went down a bit, then flew, flew, flew high into the sky. He soared into the clouds, over the mountains, far away from the dust of the barnyard. He was free, soaring, diving, gliding on wind currents, looking down at the Earth below, flying wherever he wanted to go. He was free. He was now an eagle."

I ended the story and when the students finished writing it out on the blackboard, we read it together. We discussed it's meaning. I asked, "Does that mean that if you go to a high mountain and flap your arms you can fly?"

They all thought that was silly, "No, No, that's not what it means."

We talked some more then when everyone was silent I said, "Guess what my friends. You are all eagles." I pointed around the room, "and don't let anyone call you a chicken. Or worst of all, don't you think of yourself as a chicken. You are all eagles."

The elders in the back of the room smiled and left, apparently approving of the new guy. I said to the class, "Another thing you should know. That story didn't come from the United States where I'm from. It didn't come from England. No. It came from Africa. It is an African story. It is your story."

I felt great. I felt like I belonged in Ghana. I still do.

I felt even better the next day when a charming little girl came to me and said, "I really liked your eagle story. I went home and told it to my younger brother. He kept saying, 'Tell it again. Tell it again.' So, I did."

3

United We Fall

Finally, I'm in the Savannah Airport. I had been looking forward to this trip for the two months since my son invited me to meet him in Boston. He was attending a professional conference and asked if I would join him for five days of frivolity. I thought, "Five days alone with Rob. No kids, no wives? A dream come true."

I arrived at the airport two hours early. "Don't want to get stuck in traffic." The Departure sign showed that my flight to DUI was on time. One week ago, United Airlines had beaten and dragged a physician off one of their flights to make room for crew members. Despite that public display of cruelty, I was still confident of my flights because I had never had significant trouble before.

I walked to security. The uniformed lady motioned me into her futuristic machine.

"Step on those feet markings and raise your hands like this," she said. I did. My pants fell over my pot belly. "Hitch up your pants," she said. I did. They fell again.

"Do you want me to take off my belt?" I asked.

"No, just hitch up your pants." I did. They fell again.

She flashed a twisted smile, looked at my gray hair, wrinkled face, and motioned me through. I went directly to Gate 26. The first passenger to arrive. I chuckled, "in six hours I'll be hugging Rob. Life is good."

I shrugged when half an hour before departure time an United Airlines agent announced that our flight would be delayed by twenty minutes. "No problem," I thought, but wait, this is United Airlines 2017. I went to the agent and said, "Excuse me Mam, I have only a short lay over in DUI before my flight to Boston. Do you want to reschedule me now while we have time?"

"Oh no, Sir. That won't be necessary. We expect to make up the lost twenty minutes. You should have no trouble making your connection. I sat and fidgeted along with my fellow passengers. Our plane pulled into port twenty minutes late.

"Hmm. Twenty minutes on the dot. I guess they do know what they're doing." Everyone seemed to be patient except for one fat old man. He went to the agent and occupied her time while the arriving passengers disembarked. When she finally called for us board, everyone formed a well-organized line except for that same fat old fart. He pushed his way to the front of the line, hovered over the agent, and kept demanding her complete attention, preventing everyone else from boarding. After fifteen minutes of his rudeness (I timed it), he finally boarded and we all followed. When I showed her my boarding pass, she asked, "This flight, as you know, has been delayed. "Would you like me to reschedule your Boston flight now?"

I looked behind me at the long line of anxious passengers. "No, I don't want to hold up all these good people. I'll try to reschedule in DUI." I wondered, "Why did she allow one pushy old guy to hold up all these passengers and the whole flight? Now there's no chance of any of us making our connections. We were twenty minutes late with a chance of making up the time, but now we're thirty-five minutes late and screwed.

She let that old fart bully her. SHIT. That agent, that fat old guy, and United Airlines was delaying my reunion with Rob and screwing everyone else.

We all boarded. Somehow, I was assigned seat 2A, right up front, convenient for a quick exit. I sat, pulled out my notebook, started this epistle while my blood pressure jumped. "No, I don't want any pretzels and you can keep your diet coke."

The pilot announced, "Sorry about our delay. Our flying time to DUI is one hour and twenty minutes."

I wrote to calm my nerves while resigning myself to a tardy reunion with Rob. We landed at DUI. I was the first one off the plane. An attendant asked me, "Where are you going?"

"To Boston. Gate D14."

She grabbed my arm and pointed, "Hurry, Hurry. That way. Gate 14. They're holding Flight 655 for you. Run."

I never questioned whether this old body could withstand a long sprint through a crowded airport. I thought only of Rob and took off, limping, dodging anyone in the way, determined. Gasping, staggering, laughing, I approached the shuttle flashing the remaining seconds, 14,13, 12, I had made it. I boarded the shuttle and without delay taken to Gate 14. I hustled onto the plane and strutted to the completely filled Flight 655. I collapsed into my seat. I was glad to be aboard but wondered, "How can this huge airline allow one pushy passenger to hold up not only our flight to DUI but this one to Boston? Mix one inconsiderate person with an ineffective agent and two planes full of passengers, delayed."

We took off. I sat back and focused on five days in Boston with my son. I loosened my seatbelt, the stewardess flashed me her smile, the sun radiated in through the window.

"Yes, I'll have those pretzels and water. No ice, please. 'I LOVE UNITED AIRLINES. THANK YOU, UNITED AIRLINES. I LOVE YOU UNITED AIRLINES."

4
Flashlight

Throughout my adolescence I was unable to talk to a girl. If a girl entered my space, like a sixth-grade classroom, my mind focused only on her, nothing else. I couldn't breathe normally, in and out, couldn't push the air out of my lungs, over my vocal chords, no sound, just panic. I was paralyzed by her beauty, mysticism, and the ease with which she dominated my mind.

I was jealous of my male friends, Peter, Billy, and John when they talked casually about their "spin the bottle" games with Marilyn Dunn Becky Smyth, or Betty Furman. Marilyn stole my heart by being the first eleven-year-old to wear lipstick. Becky was the first to develop breasts and enjoyed the power of her cleavage over an innocent boy like me. "What are you staring at Charles?" she asked one day. I continued staring at her femininity but couldn't force a sound. She flashed a self-satisfied smile and strutted away, swaying her tantalizing, prominent posterior.

I progressed to eighth grade at Monroe High School and left PS #49 in my wake. Although I was now a full grown high school guy, I received a birthday party invitation from a seventh grader, Darlene LaRue.

When I knocked on her front door for the party I kept telling myself, "Relax, Charles, you're an eighth grader, these girls are mere elementary schoolers. You're their macho hero."

Mrs. LaRue answered the door, giggled, and led me to her basement stairway. I descended and found the juvenile seventh grade boys and girls already paired off. Sandy Shaller was the only unattached girl. She directed me to sit in an easy chair and then promptly sat on my lap. By that time, I was getting constant erections when alone at home, but all this was happening so fast, there was zero sexual arousal.

"Sit down," she ordered and I obeyed like a PFC in boot camp.

Sandy was slightly overweight, not fat, plain looking, not ugly, and with the charm of a rabid dog. I looked around the room at some of the more desirable ladies but realized that Sandy and I were a couple and I would have to remain faithful to her through my first necking party. From across the room, Bobby Frasier yelled advice, "Charles, take a deep breath."

I did, the lights went out and Sandy Shaller kissed me right on the mouth. It was awful, like kissing a night crawler before threading it on a fish hook. I thought, "Is this what all that fear, joy, mystery, enchantment is all about?" I repressed the urge to spit. I was relieved when someone clicked on his flashlight signaling that we should stop kissing and share the wonder.

Sandy asked, "How was that?"

I told my first lie to a woman, other than my mother or a sister of course, "Gee, that was great." I was contrasting this disappointing reality with the vivid visions of Marilyn Monroe and Liz Taylor that I had conjured up in the privacy of my bedroom.

Everybody giggled and bragged about how great this is until, "Damn," the flashlight clicked off again. The room dark, more kissing, another flash, more bragging, then a welcomed flick on of the flashlight. I noticed Johnny Archibald actually licking his lips like his kisses were tasty, like an ice cream cone. Of course, the always cute Betty Furman was kissing him, not Sandy Shaller.

With each flashlight break, Sandy asked, "Wasn't that great?"

I felt like Pinocchio's brother when I answered, "Wow, it sure is. I'm having a great time. Speaking of time, I wondered what time it was and if I was going to miss tonight's episode of, "The Adventures of the Lone Ranger." Hi Ho Silver. Get 'em up Scout."

When will this necking flashlight party be finished and I can be released from this kissing nightmare? It got worse. Sandy was gaining confidence and had the nerve to stick her tongue in my mouth. That about did it for me but even then, I was too much of a gentleman to protest. "Mmm," I muttered, when I really felt like yelling, "Help! Somebody! Anybody! Help! Sandy just stuck her tongue in my mouth." Instead, I remained silent, except for a polite, "Mmm. Mmm."

My silent plea for God's help was answered when the cellar lights went on.

Thank you, God. Sandy rose from our easy chair, I jumped up and my leg cramped. I staggered toward the stairway, pulled myself up by the hand rail, and the circulation returned to my lower body.

I bid adieu. "Thanks, great party," and ran home.

I'm not sure Sandy and I ever spoke again.

I do remember that I missed "The Lone Ranger," but arrived home just in time to tune the Philco to, "True Detective Mysteries."

I slept well that night; no sexy dreams.

5

Following the Wrong Friend

Jimmy Brennan, Graham Rice and I were constant boyhood friends. Other boys filled out the baseball, football, basketball teams but the three of us lived on the same street so were always together. Jimmy was one year older than I and Graham one year younger. Jimmy was the biggest and talked the most so became our natural leader. He chose time, place, and what sport we'd play on which day. Graham and I were quieter, smaller, and less aggressive so fell in line behind Jimmy. "Come on you guys. We're playing baseball today. Chuck, you can play shortstop, Graham you play left field. I'll pitch."

Graham and I took our positions without protest. It had become an established pattern, a habit and as long as we could play baseball, we were satisfied. One Saturday Jimmy told us we were going downtown to a movie. Our leader had spoken so we did the natural thing and fell in line. He was the first one on the Rochester bus, pointed out which seat we'd take, and carried all conversations. He also picked the movie and where we'd sit in the theatre.

I was maturing slowly and starting to realize that I was no longer happy being around him and. was often more comfortable being alone with Graham. I was also old enough to see signs of meanness and cruelty in Jimmy.

Midway through "Rio Bravo," starring John Wayne, I left my seat to go to the bathroom. When I came out of the restroom, Jimmy was waiting in the hallway. He said, "I'm bored with that movie and I really don't like Graham any more. Come on Chuck, let's play a joke on that idiot. We'll leave the theater now and take the bus home without him. He's a creep."

Without protesting, I followed. I felt guilty and sick right away but at that age was unable to break away from my obsequious behavior.

I couldn't utter a sound on the way home. Jimmy continued his endless jabbering while I hung my head. "Are you Okay? Jimmy asked. I was too angry and guilty to do anything but sulk and feel very bad about myself.

I was too ashamed to tell my parents or sisters about my day at the movies. That night in bed I kept seeing my friend Graham, alone, crying on the bus home. He and his family soon left the neighborhood but that shame stayed with me. Jimmy remained a neighbor but went to a Catholic School while I went to number 49 Public School. After that horrible day at the movies, I drew away from Jimmy and never again followed or respected him. That was sixty-six years ago and when I think of that childhood incident, I still wonder how I could've been so weak as to not stick up for a friend who was being bullied.

6
Local Remedies

I was due at a play rehearsal and didn't want to disappoint my friends. I felt terrible. My nose ran, my neck was sore from violent sneezing, and, worst of all, a crippling headache. My self-diagnosis is that I have a problem with mold and mildew but no one in the medical community agrees with me. I drove the one mile to First African Baptiste Church for the rehearsal. A few people were waiting in the parking lot; the doors weren't opened yet.

I approached a close friend Cora, she has deep Gullah roots on Hilton Head and is a valued friend. I stumbled to her. "Cora, I'm sick. I have this migraine type headache and have to go home. I can't stay."

She gave me a sorrowful look. "Charlie, you go home. Don't worry. Where does your head ache?"

I told her "all over," and that I had been to neurologists, allergists, and many doctors and none had been able to really help me. She listened then spoke, "Charlie, go to the health food store and get yourself some bee pollen. Local bee pollen."

I had heard of that remedy before but sort of laughed it off and never gave it a try. She continued, "I used to get Migraines. It's related to your sinuses." she pointed above her nose to the sinus area. "My nose would run. I'd get laid down with headaches. No more. Go get bee pollen, just a couple of drops on your tongue. It'll work."

She was so confident that I had to try. As I drove away, I thought of the doctors who gave me MRIs and every blood test possible but were still confused whether my problem was sinus or migraine. Their prescription medications had limited benefit. I drove to the health food store and asked the lady behind the counter, "Do you have any bee pollen?"

She smiled as if to say, "Of course we do. We couldn't do without it." She did say, "Look behind you." A shelf was stocked with the glass jars filled with the tiny pollen granules. I have been taking it now for a week and have not had a headaches nor runny nose so far.

This incident reminded me of a safari I took with my daughter to Tanzania. We were traveling with about fourteen other tourists and one vibrant lady would occasionally have to sit out some of the activities because of a painful, red skin rash on one of her legs. This day we were all going on a hike but she sat, "I can't go. Look at my leg. It's so painful. It feels a little better when I sit and don't walk."

As I was standing above her looking down at her wretched leg, a Masi warrior stood behind. He looked at her leg and his eyes bulged. He spoke no English but pointed at the woman's sore then back to his chest indicating, I think, that he wanted to help. He was smiling like a teenager with a secret I asked my sitting companion, "What do you think? Do you want him to try?"

She said, "Oh yes. I have been to half the doctors in the states. They've all tried but none can really help me." I nodded to the tall African and he took off into the dense forest surrounding our camp. She told me, "Usually I just sit, wait, and some days that makes it feel better for a while and some days it doesn't."

We waited for a few minutes when our new Masi friend came trotting back with his long spear in one hand and carefully holding a leaf with some white salve in the other. He took great care in protecting the white substance that probably came from the sap of a special tree. He pointed to the salve then to the woman's leg indicating his intention to help. She extended her leg, inviting him to try. He took a small smear and gently applied it to her sore area.

She said, "Hmm, that does feel good." She extended her leg again, signaling for him to continue. He applied the rest of his ointment and the lady's frown turned to a broad smile. "That really does feel good. I'm amazed. Nothing has had a reaction like this before."

We continued our safari together for another week and during that time, she didn't again complain about her leg. I never saw her after our week together, but would certainly like to know how long the Masi medicine lasted. Was it a cure? I don't know.

I have tremendous respect for western medicine. I am alive today because of the treatment I received for a serious illness but I am also ready to listen to alternate remedies like bee pollen and sap from a jungle tree for whatever malady lurks in my future.

It's time now for some yoga, tai chi, and maybe a healthy shot of Highland Scotch.

7
MLK, Maya, Mitchellville

It's Martin Luther King Holiday. No school, no teaching for me. An easy morning at home with breakfast of one garlic stuffed olive, a bunch of red grapes washed down with two pints of warm water. I'll glance at the paper before heading out to meet Dick and march with hundreds of others in the MLK Parade. I have marched in every one of the twenty years since moving to Hilton Head. It feels good to acknowledge Dr. King and every year I make a new friend. It's a good day, a relaxing day.

The phone rings. Lorrie tells me Corina, from the Literacy Center is calling.

"Charlie, are you coming? You have students waiting."

"Corina, it's a holiday. I thought our classes were cancelled."

"We're here Charlie. Fanny and Aurora and LI, from China are here."

I look at the clock, 9:10. I think of Dick, then Fanny. "Corina, I'll be right there. Ten minutes. Have them write a paragraph about Martin Luther King. I'll be right there."

I give my teeth a cursory brush, try to pat down the cowlicks on my thinning hair and head for the door. Lorrie interrupts, "Charlie, you're not going to the Literacy Center looking like that, Are you?" Sometimes I don't hear my darling wife when she speaks.

In five minutes, I burst into the classroom. "I'm sorry. I'm sorry. I thought we were closed." I write new words, "Frantic," and "Frenetic," on the blackboard to explain my mood and behavior. I fill my cup with instant Maxwell House. "Gotta' have my coffee, even if it's instant. Did you write anything about Martin Luther King?" I ask.

Fanny says, "I wrote something but not about him. Do you remember, Charlie, last week? You said, 'See you Monday. Write something about the Mayans.'"

Now I have another thing to feel guilty about. I forgot my own homework assignment. In our ESL class, we have been reading about ancient Mexico with the Mayans, the Olmecs, and the Aztecs. We read mostly

American History but Aurora and Fanny are both from Mexico and we all also enjoy reading about their country.

Fanny is one of my favorites. She is about forty years old, has four children' three in school and one too young for school. She has black eyes, dark skin, a ready smile, and an enthusiasm for learning. She comes to class every day, does her homework, and is a curiosity about her new country and culture. She is a valued friend.

"Fanny, why don't you read the essay you wrote about the Mayans?" When they write, I have them read their two or three paragraphs then we all work together to help the writer with necessary corrections. She reads, while we all listen. She gets to the sentence, "The Mayans understood mathematics and astronomy and had their own written language They constructed pyramids and chapels."

I stop her there because I have just learned something myself. "Fanny, I didn't realize they had their own system of hieroglyphics."

"Yes, they write, err… wrote, excuse me Charlie. They needed know about the stars, so put pyramids in good position. Stars related to calendar."

"They even had a calendar way back then?" I ask.

"Yes, they have."

Now I'm getting excited. Everyone knows about their human sacrifice, something very negative, but few know about their advanced civilization and contributions to later cultures. I don't know why it is so important to the stronger military nations, i.e., Europeans, to obliterate the positive aspects of conquered nations.

Aurora adds, "Yes they have advanced civilization way before Europeans came." She is also proud of her Mexican heritage and wrote her own essay about the subject. She enjoys all history, Mexican and American. She loves to learn.

Both are Catholic and know the Bible stories.

I add a little kerosene to the fire. "Remember in the Bible, the Old Testament, when Abraham was ready to sacrifice his son Isaac? That too is human sacrifice, but it doesn't categorize our whole culture or religion."

No response. I avoid religious discussions so quickly change the subject.

"Fanny, you're here every day. Today is a school holiday so where are your kids?"

Before she answers Aurora excuses herself, "I need pick up son. Leave early."

"Okay Aurora. Thanks for coming. See you Wednesday."

I repeat my question, "Fanny, where are your kids? It's a holiday."

"All of them outside, in car. Wait for me to finish class."

"Fanny, do you mean that three of your kids, plus your Momma are waiting outside in the car for two hours, while you sit here in class." She gives me a strange look as if to say, "Of course Charlie. I need to learn English."

"Fanny, your attitude, your family's attitude, makes me want to do whatever I can to help you." I swallow a lump in my throat. "Fanny, we've talked about Mitchellville before."

"Yes, I remember."

"Well there is a park about two miles away. There is plenty of room for your family to run around. There are also plaques telling about Mitchellville history. It happened right here on Hilton Head and has been hidden from our own history books. Similar to Mayan history it has been left out of our history books. It, too, is important. They had their own schools, stores, police department. As a matter of fact, the first required school up until sixteen years of age in South Carolina was right here, in Mitchellville, on Hilton Head."

I think of her kids, her curiosity, our nation's history, MLK, the Mayans.

"Why don't you get in your car. I'll get in mine and you follow me to Mitchellville Park. We can read the plaques together, practice your English, and let your kids run around. They can learn something too."

"That's fine Charlie. You are doing me a favor. Let's go."

8

Being Taught by Students

Savannah is from China. She once told me her given name which I immediately forgot. At my mature age, I have enough trouble remembering "Tom. Peter or John," without the added confusion of a foreign name. I imagine when she first came to the area and her plane landed in Savannah, Georgia, she thought, *Oh Savannah sounds so pretty. That will be my American name. Savannah, I like.*

In China, she had been taught English the proper way. She knew the definition of gerund, past participle and all the other confusing terminology that we were all taught in elementary school and have long forgotten. She needed a lot of help with pronunciation, saying "rent," like "lent."

She came to the USA so her teenage son could learn to play tennis and attend Hilton Head Prep. Savannah is very proud of her country and enjoys educating the class about Chinese culture. In my class, I encourage students to write a page or two for homework then we begin each day helping each other with corrections. I soon realized that Savannah had writing talent and a wonderful sense of humor. I was surprised when she missed class for two weeks. When she returned she wrote an essay explaining her absence. I will paraphrase:

My son Frankie got very sick. Hilton Head Hospital sent him to Savannah Hospital. He there for a week get better, I bring him home, then take him back to doctor after home for week. I tell his doctor everything they do in Savannah Hospital. Give blood, IV, rest in bed, etc. I explained all this to doctor. He interrupted and asked, "Savannah, why are you telling me all this. I was his doctor. I was there.'

She turned and mumbled to Frankie in Chinese, *"I confuse, all these white people look alike. I can't tell one from the other."*

This essay was even funnier when she read it with her Chinese pronunciations of English. I couldn't speak for ten minutes.

Another student, Adrian, is from Mexico, about thirty-five years old, full bodied not fat, smiles easily and is very intelligent. For her first months of classes, she hesitated to speak.

When I asked, "Adriana, what do you think of that?" She would give one word answers, "Yes, No, I don't know."

With time and a lot of class encouragement she began to converse with the rest of us. When she wrote her essays, I could see that she was intelligent and able to put her thoughts on paper. She is the mother of three children, including, "my leetle one."

Here is an example of her emotional writing:

Wednesday after class I had a meeting at the elementary school with my son's teacher. She told me this good news, 'Alain is very responsible, intelligent, determined, good student.'

But the best moment was when one of the teachers told me that he is so proud of me because I decided to go to take English class so I could help him with his homework. WOW!!! He is proud of me. When teacher told me that, I couldn't speak and started crying because it was magic moment.

It was one of my best days. He is really good son and student. He is my world like my other two kids. They are the reason for my life. I am very proud Mom.

Here is another entry from this loveable, loving, treasured friend:

Yesterday I took my first class of math. Fractions were complicated for me. Every day I want to learn something new but it is hard.

My husband thinks I am too old to study, but I do this to help my children with their homework and for me too.

Adriana recently took her USA citizenship exam. She got 100% and is now a fellow American.

Now for more of Savannah's humor:

Best Time

I drive Frankie to school every morning. On the road, I usually give some advice about academics.

This morning I asked him, "Do you know what is best time for your memory in a day?"

No response.

I continued, "Morning is the best time. We learn best in this time.

No response.

I continued, "I think you should recite some vocabulary or do some math."

No response.

"Frankie! What you thinking? I tell you what should do."

"Mom, do you know my best time?"

"What is best time, Frankie?"

"When I don't have to hear your nagging. That is best time."

Here is Savannah's writes of the consequences when you live in a country without learning its language:

A friend who lived in Florida couldn't speak English and didn't want to learn. "Tuhao" is a Chinese word for someone who has a lot of money but no education. One day he bought a new car. He said, "Savanna, I want to take you for a ride." He was proud.

After several days, I met him but no new car. I asked, "How about your new car?"

"I sold it."

"What? Why?"

"I went to gas station and filled it with diesel. It broke my new car. I didn't know diesel word in English."

I have a valued collection of Savannah's treasures. She sees the humor in everyday events that go unnoticed by too many of us.

After twenty years, I still appreciate each moment helping these special friends with their new language.

9
Why I Teach, Travel, Live

I have been teaching English as a Second Language for almost twenty years at The Literacy Center. It is one of the most rewarding, fun, and informative things I have ever done. I teach two to three days a week and can't wait for my next class.

As one of our teaching exercises, I encourage students to write a few paragraphs for homework and then we help each other with the grammar, punctuation and spelling. Some are highly educated in their own countries and others have had little opportunity to attend school. These students are my friends, my heroes, and often my inspiration.

The different education levels of classes are sometimes a challenge. For example two students were very advanced, two were mid-level and the fifth, I judged, should be in a lower level class. I didn't want the more advanced students to get bored from too slow a pace or the beginning woman to get discouraged from going too fast.

One day after class, I was alone with Marie, who was behind the others. In very broken English she explained that she was from one of the poorest areas of Mexico and had only been to school for two years. I asked, "Marie, if you went to school for two years, how did you learn to read as well as you do?" I tried to encourage her, "You read pretty well."

She said, "My five older brothers. They help me. I teach myself."

With that statement, my whole attitude towards Marie changed. Instead of worrying about how she slowed the class, I thought of Abe Lincoln reading by candlelight, and I vowed to do everything I could to help this determined woman. The other four students were from Europe, had good educations, but were in my class to learn the language of their new country.

In the next class I had Marie tell them her story about her limited schooling and how she was teaching herself to read. They were all sympathetic and anxious to help. "Oh," said the woman from Ukraine, "my grandmother couldn't go to school. My Mom, her daughter taught her how. Even I help."

The Polish woman told a similar story and I could feel how we all suddenly bonded together, anxious to help Marie. Once we knew her story, we all admired her determination and looked up to her as a fellow human being who offered us the opportunity to help.

A different sort of class is Talk Time on Friday. There is no homework, no reading just conversation, hence the name "Talk Time."

Today I am especially glad to see Soli. She was a lawyer in Venezuela but here wants to improve her English enough to waitress in a restaurant. She once spoke fluent English but now remembers almost none of her second language. "What happened Soli?"

She tells the class that five years ago she was diagnosed with a brain tumor and endured several operations and chemo. She is now cancer free but, "I no remember nothing. My neurons no work."

Also in class are Max and Isabel from Honduras. To celebrate forty years of marriage, their 29-year-old son paid their passage from Honduras. He had graduated from Hilton Head High years ago and now manages a local restaurant. Isabel sheds tears of joy when she says," Manuel, he a good boy." She pushes her chest out, "I stay with my son," then gives her husband a passionate look usually reserved for young lovers, and says, "I live with Max."

Dina from Panama will return home in two weeks to teach school. I ask, "Where have you been in the US?"

"I been Savannah ... Orlando. I want go to Niagara Falls."

I chuckle, "It's freezing up there. I don't think you'd like it."

I write on the blackboard, "N-I-A-G-R-A F-A-L-L-S."

Soli interrupts, "That spell different in Spanish."

She takes the chalk and correctly spells 'N-I-A G-A-R-A" and sits down. I check her correct spelling on the map and try to laugh off my error. I change the subject, "Dina, have you ever seen snow?"

Soli waves her hand, "I see snow. I see in my...ah... how you say…ah…refrigerator. Every day I see snow in my refrigerator. I need new one."

Her sense of humor can turn a classroom into a comedy show. She checks her iPad and reminds us that Valentine's Day is approaching. She puts on her sad face and continues, "I wish my husband treat me better. He say me a Drama Queen."

I rise from my chair, "Soli, look straight ahead."

She does and I stoop to give her a kiss on the cheek. "Happy Valentine's Day, Soli." I give a kiss and receive a warm, gushing smile. I would make that trade any day, any time.

Class is over. I stand in the hallway as the students file past. Isabel wipes away another tear, "My son Manuel. He have a good soul."

10

Heather's Parent's Weekend

She had left home two months ago and I was desperate to see her again. Rob had left our Cape Cod home the year before to attend Wake Forrest University. One year later, Heather followed him south to Emory University.

One way I coped with the "Empty Nest Syndrome," was to look forward to her Parent's Weekend. I had never been to Atlanta so agreed that she should plan the whole weekend. "Heather, you know me. I don't want to spend a lot of money on a fancy hotel. Just some place clean, convenient and cheap."

Heather consulted with her roommate Hallet, who was from the Atlanta area.

I received a call a few days later. "Dad, Hallet was going to put her parents in this downtown hotel. They don't want to stay there so it's available."

"Sounds good Heather. How much is it?"

"I think it's only $48 per night. What do you think?"

"Wow. Sounds perfect. See you in a few days."

A week later, Heather, flashing her characteristic smile picked me up at the Atlanta Airport.

We laughed, hugged, and I shed a few tears, "Heather you look great. I guess Emory agrees with you."

"It does Dad. I can't wait to show you around. I'll Introduce you to my friends; you'll see."

We had to pass by my hotel on the way to the campus so I suggested we stop there first and check it out.

Our conversation quieted as she drove into a seedy section of Atlanta. We followed her map quest instructions to the Seneca Intown Hotel. The facade was a disorganized combination of cement block and rotting wood. There was a front door but no windows. I chuckled to see her mouth and eyes wide open in apparent shock. "Dad, you can't go in there. Let's get your money back. We'll find somewhere else."

"Heather, this is an adventure. It's cheap" I said. "Your roommate's family picked it out. I want to at least see inside."

"Dad, Hallet's parents never did see the place. This is awful. Let's get out of here."

25

"No way. The city is mobbed this weekend. This may be my best option. Come on. I'm going in. You've got to come with me. I'm not leaving you alone in the car."

We rang a bell by the front entrance and walked in. There was one small, chandeliered light hanging behind the check in desk. The muscular man behind the counter looked at us strangely, butted his cigarette in an overflowing ash tray, "Can I help you?" he asked.

"Yes, I'm Charlie McOuat. I believe I have a reservation for two nights. I'd like to check in."

He stared at me, then at my daughter. "Will she be with you the whole time?"

"Oh no. She won't be here at all. Just me."

He kind of shook his head, scratched the end of his nose with his forefinger and didn't say a word.

I broke the uneasy silence, "Can we see the room, Please?"

More silence then he asked, "How old did you say she is?"

I didn't understand the relevance of the question. "She's eighteen. She's my daughter."

He grinned, his eyes narrowed. He reached behind him for a large key with a well-worn leathery strap bearing our room number 21.

"Where's the elevator?"

"There is none. The stairs are over there."

I turned and almost tripped over a wrinkled throw rug. A dim, shadeless light bulb guided us up the ragged, rubber padded stairway. Posts were missing from the banister. Decaying plaster hung from the walls and ceiling; our eyes strained to find the faded number 21. I turned the key, pushed in the door, and ushered Heather inside. The exuberant, happy expression that greeted me at the Atlanta Airport had now turned to a frightful face that I remembered from her childhood horror stories.

I flicked on the light switch exposing a single bulb hanging from the ceiling by a wire wrapped in duct tape. The only bed, slightly wider than a cot, was partially covered with a ripped, well-worn sheet. The pillow was gray from sweat and experience. The whole room stank of stale beer and cigarettes. Uncovered piping supported a filthy sink jutting out from the wall beside the bed. Three tiny remnants of soap nestled in the bottom of the scum laden bowl. I pushed aside a curtain that led to a shower adorned with matching soap fragments and a commode that looked scrub brush starved.

"Dad, let's get out of her. This is the pits."

"Heather, chill out. I hate to tell you this. Don't take it personally. On your first Parent's Weekend ever, you have arranged for your innocent Papa to spend two nights in an Atlanta whore house."

She looked around, her cheeks filled with air, her head shot back and her stifled giggle erupted into a full, uncontrolled, riotous laugh. "Really?" I hugged her as we surveyed our surroundings. We were both out of control, appreciating the humor of the oft used room that had become less threatening and more comedic as we realized its purpose.

My lodging was a constant joke through our wonderful weekend together.

I stayed both nights at the Seneca Intown Hotel, but never unpacked my bags, slept both nights with my clothes on with my head resting on my backpack instead of the soiled pillow. I never used the shower nor commode.

And NO, I did not indulge in the professional service offered by the hotel.

11

Stan the Man, Resurrected

A week ago, I spent an afternoon cleaning out my desk drawer. I throw temporary treasures into it, let them lie for at least a decade, but seldom pull anything out. I found a sampling of my Letters-to-the-editor, photos of me in the HH Island Packet, and miscellaneous clippings that were so important for a very short time.

I reminisced. The only treasure worth any money was a silver dollar from the 1920s. I took it immediately to the local jeweler, who offered the exorbitant price of $27.'It's a deal," I responded, pushing the gem across the counter before he changed his mind.

I have already written two stories about one of the highlights of my childhood when the Rochester newspaper photographed me getting Stan Musial's autograph. I kept that photo of Stan and me through college years, the U.S. Army, and two moves during my professional life. It turned up missing when we moved to Hilton Head twenty years ago.

Last week, while digging in the drawer, I found it. It was faded, yellowed, crumpled but a true buried treasure. I thought of all the people I had mentally accused of trashing that newspaper clipping.

Topping that list of suspects was Susan Person. Her name, I'm sure, is no longer Person and I have no interest in finding her to apologize for wrongly accusing her for Stan's disappearance. After Marilyn's death, Susan and I dated for two traumatic years, married for one week, divorced, and have gone one with our separate lives since 1982. She knew how much I valued that clipping. Our fights were full of venom, vengeance, and emotionally draining. I thought Stan's photo would be another way for her to get back at me. Sorry Susan, glad you didn't do it. I wish you the best in your life.

Suspect number two was a boarder in my old house on Cape Cod. He was a real live bad guy. After a few months in the house, he stopped paying rent, did his best to wreck the house, and refused to move out when I asked him to. The sheriff had to evict and it cost me thousands of dollars to repair the damages after he vacated. He was bad and capable of doing anything to get back at me. I won't apologize for blaming him. I'm sure he is making someone's life miserable today. No apology there.

The third person who I blamed for Stan's destruction was me, Charlie McOuat. I was organized in my dental days, thanks to my assistants and my own desire to do a good job. Since the day I retired, my natural self has erupted. I have been careless, disorganized, messy, etc. I'm sure Lorrie would have more graphic adjectives to describe my behavior in retirement.

My photo of Stan and me is now tucked away safely in 13 Outpost Lane. *Hmm, now that I'm thinking of it, where did I put it? It's either in my bedroom or my man cave. Or is it on the porch? It's definitely in the house…. somewhere*

12

The Ghost of the Widdah

We had just arrived in Orleans for four days of reunions with the old friends who were still alive and somewhat lucid. Both Lorrie and my families grew up in this small Cape Cod fishing village that was now a tourist hot spot. We were looking forward to our evening dinner with the Hartung's but first headed to the traditional drinking spot, "The Land Ho," for lunch.

As I maneuvered our rented jeep into a parking space, Lorrie said, "Oh look! Over there, that truck...err boat....err whatever it is. What is it?" Parking in front of us was a boat, truck, pirate ship, work of art, jockeying into the prime Land Ho parking place.

Unusual sights and crazy people attract me so I jumped out of our car and walked briskly to the mystery vehicle. As I approached, I could see that it was a truck body with a wooden pirate ship cleverly built over and around the chasse making it an amphibious masterpiece. I stood at the front where huge intimidating teeth had replaced the grill work. The ship was painted completely in bright reds, blues, violets, and yellows to stimulate the curiosity of all onlookers. I gawked.

Perched on top of this treasure was a huge sign, "Ghost of the Whydah." The Whydah was an 18th century ship, captained by the notorious Sam Bellamy that went down to its salty graveyard off Cape Cod supposedly loaded with pirated gold and Spanish doubloons. The legend persisted until Cape Cod diver and archeologist Barry Clifford discovered the wreck, with its treasure intact in 1985. It is the only pirate shipwreck discovered and authenticated in the world.

I inched closer to the rebuilt Whydah. I marveled at the creativity of the owner and chuckled as the ghost of Sam Bellamy climbed out of his truck/ship. Long black pigtails dangled from his red head wrap. A gruesome black cape draped over his menacing figure and two "guns" protruded from a wide leather belt. His boots jingled as he strutted towards me. Lorrie, sensing something she did not want to get involved in, excused herself. "Charlie, I'm going to Shirley's shop. I need to buy a blouse for tonight's dinner." My faithful darling left me alone to confront the pirate. I took a step back and studied his expressionless face while he glared back at my wrinkled skin and gray hair. The corners of his mouth turned upwards as he growled, "Arrgh, Arrgh." I assumed that underneath the disguise lurked a misunderstood, friendly pirate.

I looked closer at his face, his build, and thought of a long-ago friend who might be able to create such a treasure. I asked, "Are you by any chance Jerry Honeycutt?"

He became serious, "Who are you?"

I now recognized the sound of his voice and his face hidden under the pirate makeup. "I'm Charlie McOuat."

He gave a broad grin, "Yeh, Charlie it's me, Jerry. Avast Lad, you haven't changed a bit," he lied

I laughed, we hugged, and I made no attempt to control my exuberance, "Come on. I need to buy you a drink." I draped my arm over his shoulder and steered him into the always welcoming Land Ho.

It was midafternoon but the darkened restaurant was crowded with locals and vacationers from all over the world. It seemed like every face snapped towards us as we walked into the bar area. A small girl left her family table to get a closer look at the colorful intruder. Jerry bent over, smiled at the adolescent, and left his calling card with the family. I took a seat at the bar and admired pirate Sam's ghost working the room.

My explosive guffaw drew some attention away from the pirate. "Jerry, come on. Let me buy you a beer."

"Arrgh," he answered, "I'll have rum, Matey."

The bartender brought my Guinness and his rum. "Jerry, how long has it been? The last thing I remember was that you made these bird feeders that fit into people's windows. There was one-way glass or something so the feeder came right into the room. People loved it and you couldn't make them fast enough. I lost track. What happened?"

"It's true, I couldn't make them fast enough. L.L. Bean bought them out and that ended the feeders."

"Jerry, I will always remember the night that you and Diane, Marilyn and I were out together and Diane rubbed some makeup or something into her eyes. She went into immediate anaphylactic shock. Her face swelled. Her throat constricted. I thought she was doomed. It scared me half to death. I remember the ride to the hospital. We were all panicked."

"You remember that? Diane. That had to be thirty years ago."

"It was more than that. Marilyn was still alive. It was almost forty."

"Probably was. How old are you?"

"I just turned seventy-five. And you?"

"I got ya by two years. I'm seventy-seven." I was surprised because despite his outfit, I viewed him as unchanged from forty years ago. Seeing an old friend at my favorite old-time watering hole made me morph into Peter Pan, the boy who never grew older. This Orleans bar had turned into Never Land and Jerry was now Captain Hook and not the local pirate legend, Sam Bellamy. Our reunion had set the clock back and I wasn't ready to come back to reality when Lorrie returned from shopping.

She saw us laughing and reminiscing but brought me further back from Never Land to Orleans, Mass. 2016, when she stated, 'Charlie, we've got to get back to the motel. I've got to shower and get ready for the Hartungs. Are you ready?"

I chugged my Guinness. "Come on Lorrie. Give my pirate friend a big hug and we'll be on our way." Jerry handed us each his business card. There he was in full regalia standing beside his pirate ship/truck, and his email, *thedancingpirate.com*. "I write and produce songs to create music schools on a 150' schooner for veterans. It's a nonprofit. As Capt. Black Strapp Molasses, I've written 'Ghost of the Whydah Pirate Song,' and 'Captain's Got Good Times Syndrome.'"

I couldn't stop hugging my long lost, dancing pirate, performer, producer, inventor, song writer, friend, Jerry.

Lorrie and I leaned on each other as we made our way from the Land Ho to the car.

Thomas Wolfe said, "You can't go home again." I can. If I didn't go home again, I'd miss Jerry, the Hartungs, Squires, Erhardts, O'Haras, Leonards and so many other precious people who made me what I am today. People who stood by me in hard times, who encouraged, mentored, modeled, and made me laugh so many, many times. I thank them all with deepest love.

13

Leo Tolstoy, Brian, and "You Get What you Deserve

One of the characteristics of the aging process is evaluating life, thinking seriously about an afterlife and paying attention to other people's biographies.

One of my favorite authors is Leo Tolstoy, often considered the best, at least one of the best, authors of all time. Years ago, I read his *War and Peace, Anna Karenina,* and most of his shorter creations. Recently, I read his *Resurrection*, which is autobiographical. After Tolstoy became world famous and wealthy beyond imagination, he struggled for thirty years with serious depression and constant fixation on suicide. In *Resurrection,* he wrote about his own destructive obsessions while reporting on his observations of Russian society, their law and penal system, and his disappointment with the Orthodox Church. He was eventually excommunicated from the church, discredited by the government, while struggling with his own inner turmoil.

He felt guilty about his lofty, privileged position while so many others suffered in poverty, unjustly jailed or exiled to Siberia. Their lives were hopeless, with unending misery. By observing and writing about their lives, he suffered personal despair. Before publishing *Resurrection in 1899,* he had an epiphany, like Paul on the road to Damascus. For him the healing came from HOPE, not through the church, but his personal link with God.

He reported on many serfs and other dissatisfied Russians who were refusing to take an oath to serve in the military. They were like our "conscientious objectors." He believed that this was a significant change spreading through his country and the world. He expected that these brave souls would free the world from war, violence, and injustice.

This comes from one of the great thinkers of modern times. He wrote *Resurrection* in 1898. I assume he was unaware of the carnage going on in other parts of the world, like the Boer War in South Africa and the Spanish American War in our hemisphere, Russia was soon to be humiliated by the Japanese in their Russian- Japanese War 1904-1905 and have its own bloody revolution in 1918. Following soon after that were the crescendos of World Wars I and II. He died in 1910 before confronting the failure of peace in our times.

I enjoyed Tolstoy's R*esurrection* and his optimism about his late-in-life belief in man's inherent goodness.

Those lofty hopes would have been shattered if he had lived long enough to witness scenes of the Holocaust, the Rape of Nanking, the butchery of Pol Pot, Stalin, Hitler, etc., etc., etc.

On a more personal level, I like everyone, have had many challenges in my life. Now at age 76 I see that this suffering is part of the human condition. I have valued friend named Brian. We have written together for maybe ten years. We have tried to listen, encourage, help, prod each other through life's challenges. Last Thursday he joked that "You only get what you deserve." I burst out laughing. In other words, "We only suffer because we are all BAD, sinful people.

He again joked, "I wish you could all be Catholic for one day. Just 24 hours, that's all."

We all laughed as we left our Barnes and Noble meeting place. Our hour together and my recent exposure to Tolstoy made me smile and scowl at realism. I thought of Rabbi Kushner's book, "Bad Things Happen to Good People."

I am no closer to a valid explanation of this "human condition" than the great Count Leo Tolstoy was more than a century ago.

14

A Profession Demanding Perfection

I was in a profession that demanded perfection. If I was crowning someone's tooth, I would prepare that tooth in a perfect way, take a perfect impression, and send it to the lab where a technician would have to make a perfect crown. When I tried it in the patient's mouth, it had to fit 100% or it was no good. If the cap covered 99% of the tooth and 1% was exposed, it had to be done over: a new impression, back to the lab, another try-in.

When I extracted a tooth, if a piece of the root broke off, I was responsible for digging out the pieces. It was not permissible to leave the smallest bit of root tip in the patient's mouth. I was lucky. After dental school, I served for two years in the US Army at Fort Jackson in Columbia, South Carolina. From 1968-1970 I went to work at the base clinic, from 8 AM to 5PM, just like a regular job. I did a lot of extractions on recruits and was fortunate to work closely with an excellent Oral Surgeon who taught me the easiest and proper way to dig out broken teeth from the soldiers, who were probably headed for Vietnam. I entered the Army as a dentist with little experience and not much confidence in my skills. The Army was great for me. When I left, and went into private practice with another dentist in a small town in the Adirondack Mountains, I was confident especially when doing extractions. After two years, I left Cobleskill and opened my own practice. Extracting teeth was a small part of dentistry on Cape Cod, but I continued doing them and other dentists even referred some of their difficult extractions to me. Thanks to the Army, I knew how to shake a tooth in a certain way to minimize chances of breaking off pieces and if they did break, I knew how to remove bone and retrieve small pieces from the socket.

In 1983, a friend asked if I would like to go to Haiti for two weeks to do dentistry. I had never been to a developing country but knew that "doing dentistry," in Haiti would be limited to extractions. No crowns, root canals or even fillings, just extractions. I worked in two different "clinics," neither of which had any equipment. I had brought my own forceps, elevators, probes, needless and anesthetic carpules. In the mountain town of Plaisance, a young man had been yanking teeth with pliers and no anesthetic. I showed him how to administer Novocain and all I knew about extractions. The patients sat in a rickety wooden chair, an assistant held a flashlight so I could see (somewhat) and I did the extractions. Some of the patients were severely infected with swollen jaws and fistulas, or pus tracks, draining from their cheeks. What is a toothache and temporary pain in our country was a life-threatening condition for these unfortunate Haitians. I had never felt so needed or proud to put my professional training to use as I did for those two weeks.

A problem was, that many of these patients had difficult extractions and if a root broke off, I had no choice but to tell them what happened and wish him well. I felt good about my services in Haiti, even returned two years later. However, I never was able to deal with the guilt that I came away with from leaving broken pieces of tooth in the patient's mouth. Perfectionism did not work in Haiti. I had to learn to accept my own limitations and feel grateful that I could help in some way.

I had a strong desire to live and work in a developing country after my two kids left for college. While I was still practicing in Orleans I commuted to Boston University to earn a Master's Degree in Public Health. I hoped to live and work in a developing country in some non-dental way. Instead, I got remarried, retired, and moved to Hilton Head with Lorrie.

My desire to live in a developing country never left me. When a Rotarian friend asked if I'd like to go to the West African country of Ghana to give polio immunizations, I jumped at the chance. I spent two weeks giving polio immunizations and then when the Rotarians came back to America, I taught school in the small mountain village of Biakpa. No root tips, no professional compromise, no guilt, just teaching. I loved it and returned three more times to teach in Biakpa and in an orphanage in Accra.

Two years ago, I was taking a break from a health club in Hilton Head and had a friendly chat with a retired Oral Surgeon. He was contemplating a mission trip to Africa. I told him about my Haitian experience and how I sometimes had no choice but to leave broken root fragments in a patient's mouth. He said, "If you've never left a root tip, you've never done extractions." In other words, sometimes it is better for the patient to tell them about the situation than to drill away huge amounts of their jaw bones to retrieve a tiny root fragment that will probably never be a problem.

I am a non-perfectionist in a profession that demanded perfection. I'm glad I was a dentist but very glad to be retired.

Now my wife will too often point out imperfections like weeds in our garden that "Should be pulled." I can smile and say "Ah, It's good enough." Or she'll tell me that my hair is uncombed or there is a spot on my t-shirt. I love saying, "It's good enough."

I think this writing is OK, not perfect, but "good enough."

15
Bikes and Broads

I haven't seen Helen Wicks since fourth grade at PS #49 but she has had a major influence on my life. She was one year ahead of me, could do cartwheels, stand on her head for at least ten seconds, and looked like a Hollywood sex goddess in her navy-blue gym uniform. She didn't know I existed. She liked James Stanton who was her age and could blow huge bubbles with his Fleers gum.

When I laid in bed or just sat with a quiet moment, I thought of Helen's legs, her huge smile, the soft tone of her voice when she talked with other boys. My problem was that I was so determined that she not see me making a fool of myself, that for a few crucial months, I was immobile. My father offered to teach me how to ride a bike. I refused to hop on; afraid Helen might happen by and see me fall. I told my Dad, "I don't want to ride that thing."

When I went to the school yard for a ball game, I walked or rode on Jimmy Brennan's handle bars. I did that for years until high school when bike riding was no longer the accepted mode of transportation. Biking was for kids, not for a cool high school guy. Nobody in my high school realized that I had never ridden a bike and no one cared. Helen? I think she moved away by sixth or seventh grade and some other girl took her turn twisting my brain. My life progressed without a two-wheeler.

That changed again in one of my college summers when I worked as a waiter at the White Elephant Hotel on Nantucket Island. I chose Nantucket because I loved it and also because you didn't need a car. I had none. The problem was, everyone rode bikes. Again, a woman dictated my life. The staff of the hotel were all college students, like myself. I had a paralyzing crush on the restaurant hostess, Mary Jo Butler from Florida State University. We joked, laughed, teased and flirted. Every helpless male loved her, especially me.

The collegiate staff did almost everything together. There was not much dating, just group fun. One night we were all in town drinking, laughing, singing songs, telling stories, drinking some more until it was time to go home. I had ridden in with a friend in one of the few cars in our group. Another friend with a swollen knee, couldn't ride his bike back to our dorm so he asked, "Charlie, would you please ride my bike back. My knee hurts. I need to ride in the car."

It was a simple request and without thinking, I slurred, "I don't know how to ride a bike."

Mary Jo's explosive laughter woke up even the solitary drinkers at the bar. "What did you say? Did you say you can't ride a bike?" She had a great sense of humor and was out of control.

"Yeh, I just never learned. I've never ridden one."

She caught her breath and paused long enough to say, "Charlie, what is your work schedule tomorrow?"

"I think I have lunch off. I'm just working breakfast and dinner."

She then announced to our group and the rest of the crowded bar, "Everybody. Listen. Tomorrow one o'clock. Behind the hotel. Starbuck Road. Charlie is going learn to ride a bike. He's never ridden one. Do you believe that?"

I would've done anything for Mary Jo. I went to bed with enough beer in me that I don't remembering being anxious about the next day's challenge. I think I was old enough to realize that "looking stupid," was part of my make-up and nothing out of the ordinary. By that time in my life, I had made an ass of myself with such regularity (all having to do with women) that another "stupid experience," was no problem. Besides, I'd be with Mary Jo.

I also assumed that most people would rather be on the beach than watch a twenty-year-old wrestle with a two-wheeler. I was wrong.

At quarter to one, I walked behind the hotel to the lightly traveled Starbuck side road, expecting a private lessen from Mary Jo. Instead, I was greeted by cheers, yells of encouragement and derision by at least twenty sadistic co-workers. I was the show.

Mary Jo held the bike. "Hop on." she ordered.

I did, of course. She said, "Charlie, I'm going to give you a big push. You pedal. You'll see. It's easy."

She pushed, I pedaled, I teetered. I fell. Everyone roared. "Charlie, you've got to steer. Pedal and steer," they shouted.

I did. I teetered. I swerved. I kept on pedaling, gained my balance and rode away to cheers, taunts, clapping, and roaring of the crowd.

I'm now 76 and pedal almost every day, like I was back at PS #49. Thank you, Mary Jo.

16
Circuity, Confusion, and Cayuga

Our visit to Rochester, New York was an exuberant homecoming. Lorrie and I enjoyed my sisters, cousins, nephews, my daughter Heather and her four-year-old son Mikey. We laughed, wined, dined, shed a few emotion releasing tears as we reminisced over the good and the bad times. I hadn't seen my Rochester relatives for seven years, but within a short time, we were comfortable with each other, telling stories, embellishing, exaggerating, each from our own viewpoint. The cool weather was a welcome relief from our hot, humid summer on Hilton Head.

We only had two days remaining before we returned South so I was getting restless. A rented Volkswagen Beetle provided some independence for the last two days. The Budget Rental agent said $90 which I thought was a good deal but we found out later that he had quoted $190 instead of 90. No problem. I am used to confusion like that with my hearing loss.

I wanted to show Lorrie the Finger Lakes Area and maybe my Mother's birthplace of Cayuga, New York.

I remembered a long-ago family trip to Watkins Glenn when I was a young boy. I checked a map and Lorrie consulted her cell phone GPS. We followed the NY State Thruway to Geneva, then south on route 14 to Watkins Glenn. I was proud of our teamwork as we relaxed and viewed the fantastic sights, going south along the west side of Seneca Lake. I hadn't remembered such scenery as a child but was probably too busy whining and being impatient to get to our destination.

We parked the Volkswagen about one-third of the way up the glen, thinking the whole hike would be too much for our mature bodies. We limped down a steep, stone, stairway with no handrails. Lorrie, who is less arthritic and less stiff than I am, led the way. I have become ultra-cautious on stairs because too many of our Hilton Head friends have fallen and had their lives changed forever. "Lorrie, wait at the bottom. I'll get there. I think."

She said, "Charlie those stairs are dangerous. Look at that path over there. Maybe we should take then when we go back to our car."

I panted, took a deep breath, and replied, "Good idea. We haven't even seen the glen and I'm already pooped. I think maybe I should take your advice. If I'm struggling with this, I probably should forget about a return to Ghana. I can't even do these stone stairs."

"Charlie, hallelujah, please. Every time you mention going back to Africa, I get scared."

I changed the subject, "Let's push on. It's right over there, I think." She led on to "The Indian Trail," and we began our assent to "The Falls." I checked a wall map, "Lorrie, wait a minute. Look at this. We're already gasping, stumbling and we're not even a quarter of the way to the end. Let's go back." We did an about face and returned to the car. At our mature age, we make choices and we agreed on the comfort of the car instead of the slippery, steep Indian Trail.

It was time for lunch and again luck was on our side. A man in shinny white uniform invited us aboard a well broken in ferry boat. "Come on," he said. "We give a two-hour tour of the lake and serve you a roast beef lunch along the way."

"Can't beat that," I said, "We're in." We found out later that the cost was $90 apiece, not including tip, but the views and the cruise on the largest finger lake was worth the price.

Two hours later we disembarked, with full stomachs, and wonderful memories of our Seneca Lake excursion.

We hurried back into our Beetle.

I had seen from a map at sister Flora's house that Cayuga, New York was on the east side of Cayuga Lake. I assumed we would drive north on the east side of neighboring Seneca Lake, to the New York State Thruway, turn east a few miles to the Cayuga Village exit. Unfortunately, we took a "shortcut." We were headed north on the west side of Seneca when a sign read, "Route 79 to Cayuga." I bit at the "shortcut bait." I drove with caution over the steep, curvy, beautiful hills. We drove, swerved, slowed, sped over the jacket rabbit type terrain, enjoying the exquisite views in every direction. Lorrie, who has almost perfect diction said, "We seem to be taking a "curc-weu-i-tee" route."

We both chuckled her inability to pronounce the word "circuitous." She's the one who usually corrects my mispronunciations. "Lorrie say, "Sir."

She said "Sir."

"Cue."

She said, "Cue."

"It."

She said, "It."

"Now say, 'Us.'"

She said, "Us."

"Now put it all together, 'Circuitous.'"

"Circuitous," she said slowly, distinctly, correctly.

We both chuckled, cheered, and congratulated her achievement.

We drove on, and on, and on. I said, "Lorrie, this is hilly country. We've been driving for an hour. We should be approaching Cayuga, the town, but nothing is familiar."

"Yes, Charlie, but it's been sixty-five plus years for you. Things change. A GPS doesn't lie."

"I've never heard of any of these towns. I think we're lost. I'm sure I've never been here before."

"Charlie, it says right here on my cell phone. Cayuga is only five minutes away. We're almost there. Computers don't lie you know."

"I don't trust those gadgets."

I just said those propitious words when a sign read, "Entering Ithaca." "Ithaca," I shouted, "We're at the wrong end of the lake. That damn thing took us to Cayuga Lake, not the town. We're way out of our way. We're at the south end of Cayuga Lake, not the north end. Now we have to drive the whole length of the lake to the thruway… Our circuitous route took us to the lake not the town. I hate those things."

We drove on over more roller coaster hills. I was getting discouraged until I saw a sign, "Route 96." "Lorrie, route 96, Route 96. That's the road we used to drive from Rochester to Cayuga. We must be getting closer." I could almost remember my dear father saying, "Good Old Route 96," like it was a sign of familiarity, home, our destination. I breathed easier and kept driving through unfamiliar small farming towns.

Lorrie again was the realist, "Charlie, we may have to forget the town of Cayuga and head to Rochester."

I stopped at a run down, car repair shop in a tiny, nameless village. A bearded man in overalls had his head buried under the hood of a rusted-out jalopy. "Sir, can you help me?"

He peaked out from underneath, "Yeah?"

I said, "We're trying to get to the town of Cayuga, New York." I slowly pronounced "Cay-U-Ga," so he could understand.

He looked at me head to foot, stared, laughed in a condescending, authoritative, manner. "There is no Cayuga, New York. Cayuga is a lake, not a town." He looked at me like I was the world's dumbest person. "No, sir. It's a lake, ha, ha, not a town. There is no town of Cayuga, only a lake."

I jumped back in our Beetle and headed out of the village, following the sign to Geneva, and ultimately, Rochester. "Lorrie, there is a town called 'Cayuga.' They don't erase towns just because people move away to the big city. I've heard of a town out west where there was only one person. It's still a town. That damn cell phone, GPS, has done us in again. I give up. Let's go back to Rochester. We'll find out."

I followed the route 96 signs to Geneva, then back on the Thruway, and on to Rochester. Lorrie kept reeling off the distances to the city. We sped on by Elmwood Avenue, Highland Avenue, Mt Hope, all exits that would take us directly to Flora's house. "Lorrie, we should get off at one of these. We're right here in Flora's neighborhood."

"Charlie, it says right here on my GPS, Rochester is ten miles ahead. You have to trust these things. Computers don't lie. Keep going. Exit 14."

Exit 14 was Broad St. In the center of the city.

"Lorrie, here's proof that those things are no good. You punched in Rochester, along with Laney Road, Flora's address. Now we're the center of Rochester and we have to back track to my sister's. That's how we got lost in the Finger Lakes Forrest. You punched in Cayuga and that impersonal, unreliable GPS took us to the Lake not the town I hate computers, cell phones, and GPSs. There all a 'flash in the pan.' A fad. Take me back to the old reliable road map, party lines, and signs like, "Route 96.' Those were the days."

She said, "I'm sure you'd be happier in a horse and buggy than this Volkswagen Beetle."

"Now you're talkin'. You're right. Nothing wrong with a horse and buggy. Computers, Bah Humbug."

We drove into my sister's driveway. I was more convinced than ever that cell phones, GPSs and computers would soon be part of our history. Discarded. Unreliable. A toy, like a Rubik's Cube.

17
Legalese

Lorrie and I each have two children from our first marriages. We have always agreed that anything in her name will be passed to her children, anything in my name will go to mine. That is a simple statement and we have never had a hint of conflict on that key issue.

My question is after a prenuptial agreement, wills, trust funds, countless lawyers, and domestic peace, why did a lawyer friend of mine advise, "That situation must be clarified legally. You've moved. You live in a different state."

"Yes, but we've had our wills and everything else rewritten in South Carolina."

"That's good, but you had better get this straight, now. You each need your own lawyer. Think of your kids. Consult a lawyer."

Damn. We took my friend's advice and each hired our own lawyer. After three weeks of anxiety, we finally received in the mail our signed, certified, legalized, witnessed eight-page "Modification of our Ante-Nuptial Agreement." Each paragraph on the first page began with, "Whereas," a scary legalese word meaning nothing. We read down to "Now Therefore," and Lorrie asked, "Charlie, can you tell me what this is all about?"

"No, Lorrie, I can't. We need to hire another lawyer to interpret this crap." I joked. Here is a one paragraph legal explanation of, "Whatever is mine goes to my kids, whatever is yours goes to your kids.

"Should either party become entitled at law to the estate share of the estate share of the other under provisions of the last will and testament executed prior to the date of this agreement and not ratified, confirmed or re-executed in writing after the signing of this agreement, then the surviving party shall within one month following the date of notice of the death of the other party disclaim and renounce in writing any interest whatsoever in which he or she may have in the estate of the other irrespective of any provisions to the contrary made in the will of the deceased party,"

That interminably long one sentence paragraph is only the opening salvo. It goes on for eight pages of mumbo-jumbo. Why can't our agreement be stated in clear, readable English? Any thought or idea can be stated in simple declarative sentences. Why do lawyers need to write such nonsense that the average person has to run for aspirin when exposed to their legal lingo?

Only the legal profession could write a 15,000-word document and call it a "Brief."

There are too many lawyers and they all need to pay their bills and send their kids to college. A comparison with my profession, "Dentistry," might offer a partial explanation.

I was an Army dentist from 1968-1970. This was the Vietnam War period and our country, our armed forces needed dentists, there were 500,000 brave soldiers in Vietnam and they needed dental support. To meet that need, dental schools increased in size and new ones opened. After the war ended, the demand decreased so dental school decreased their enrollments and some even closed. This was an effective way of regulating the number of dentists.

In contrast, at that same time, law schools kept increasing in size and more schools opened, resulting in the flood of lawyers that our country now has to cope with. One way for them to stay busy is for them to disregard their elementary school English lessons and develop their own legalese jargon, like the above example.

The concept of "Contingency Fee," could only come from the legal profession. A lawyer explains, "A contingency fee means that if I don't win your case, I don't get anything. If I do win your case, you don't get anything."

I rest my case.

18
Panic

I had just finished a meeting with two treasured friends. We meet once a week to read our stories together that we have written for homework assignments. Brian and I have been meeting like this for seven years and have enjoyed Merrill's contributions for at least two. We had been meeting at the scholarly Barnes and Noble Bookstore until we decided to try a new place. Our old haunt had become overcrowded and too noisy for easy communication.

We had just finished our second meeting at the local McDonald's Hamburg Restaurant. I began, "I hate to be a snob but I think we should go somewhere a little upscale from this place. The seats are comfortable, the coffee is good and cheap but I think I'd be more comfortable in a little higher-class place."

Brian agreed and then asked Merrill, "What do you think? It's clean enough here, not too noisy but the atmosphere? What do you think?"

"I agree with you both." Then he joked, "McDonald's really isn't stimulating for our SPRAWL Meetings." With false pomp, we call our casual meetings SCRAWL for South Carolina Reading and Writing League, and often add the superfluous "Guild."

We stood up, smiled at each other and agreed to return to our familiar Barnes and Noble Bookstore next week. It certainly has a more erudite atmosphere than McDonald's.

A bearded man stumbled past, reminding me that homelessness does indeed exist on Hilton Head Island. A man carrying two loads of McDonald's sugary, greasy breakfast treats proudly presented his treasure to his three daughters, all too young to attend school. I opened the exit door and made my way through a long line of impatient, hungry drivers scowling at the slow moving take out window.

I drove away leaving McDonalds and all those American voters behind while I headed to my LAVA Fitness Center. I thought, *I'm really lucky to shed that MacDust. I'll feel good again after a healthy workout.* I parked the car, reached for my gym bag, and dropped my keys into my pocket. *My pocket: Where's my wallet?* I took everything out. *No wallet. Must have slipped under the seat. I took everything off the seats, looked under papers, discarded T-shirts, and assorted car debris.* "Shit! No wallet." *I crouched under the back seat looked and underneath, both sides. No wallet, no choice, no workout today.*

I stood by the car, irrationally turning my empty pockets inside out. No wallet. Back into my GMC Terrain to drive back the restaurant. I thought, "Oh no, the dreaded Office of Motor Vehicles, the credit card shuffle. What will Lorrie say? Hmph, I know what she'll say.*

I cut off a car as I sped out of the LAVA parking lot. He swerved out of the way and tooted his horn. I didn't have time to swear back at him. *"Got to get to McDonalds."* The traffic light was turning from green to yellow. I sped up and shot through. Fortunately, no cops or slow drivers clogged the intersection. I swore at cars traveling at the legal 55 MPH speed limit on Route 278. My odometer read 60 MPH and I stepped on the gas. The left lane was open. I passed five cars, then swerved into the right lane to pass one of those "inconsiderate ass-holes," who drive the speed limit in the left lane. *Gotta get to McDonalds. A new credit card? Who issued it? What's the difference? Bank America, I think, Credit card, new ID. The horror. More gas, more swerving, more swearing.*

If I get stopped by a cop now for speeding, he'll say, "Where's the fire Mister? Driver's License Please."

"Yes, but you don't understand. I'm a good guy. Obey all the laws. I just don't have my license. I lost it."

"Out of the car, Buddy. Clasp your hands behind your back. I'm putting the cuffs on you. No license. Hello Jail."

"Yes but...."

"Shut up. Put your hands behind you. You're going to jail. You have the right to remain silent."

I came back to the present, slowed down and flicked on my left blinker to turn into McDonalds. I cut in front of an oncoming car and said a prayer. "Oh, Lord. If it be your will, please let some nice person turn in my wallet. Thy will be done...."

I entered McDonalds, where this mess, this jail sentence, the Motor Vehicle drudgery, started. There was a line of maybe eight people. *"Should I excuse myself, explain the situation, or just cut in front?"* Rationality prevailed. I stood in the back of the line, shifting my weight from one foot to the other, looking around the counter, up on the shelves but didn't see my wallet. A different woman was taking orders than the one on duty when I entered an hour ago. The woman who had waited on me was now transferring Egg MacMuffins from the burner to the plastic serving trays. *"She's still here."* I breathed easier. *"But if my wallet isn't here, should come right out and accuse her?"* Another moral dilemma.

An eternity passed before I reached the front of the line. I took a deep breath, "Good Morning. I'm Charlie.," as if that mattered. "Has a wallet been turned in here within the last hour?"

Her eyes twinkled like Santa Claus. "Yes, wait here."

I watched her disappear into a back room and return with my torn, tattered, beautiful wallet. She handed it to me with a proud smile. I looked in and saw the twenty-dollar bill still settled in place. I took it out and handed it to my new hero. She shook her head, "No," then carefully folded the twenty, corner to corner, and stuffed it in her pocket.

She beamed, but not as much as I did. I had found my wallet. Beautiful, wonderful, classy, McDonalds had come through. I looked up at the customers waiting to pick up their now, healthy, nutritious food. I was part of a brotherhood. I asked a man grinning at me, "Have you ever lost your wallet?"

"I sure have friend. I sure have."

I patted the wallet in my pocket and left the restaurant, *"What a fine establishment to have in our friendly town. I'm glad we had our two SCRAWL meetings here. What a great place this is.* Maybe I'll dine here more often. We'll see what Lorrie has to say about that."

As I read over the above SCRAWL writing assignment for this week, I think back to another time that such a hysterical state would have been appropriate, but don't think that I was as panicked

Three friends and I were white water rafting in Maine. It was an unusually hot day in early Spring. Despite the 90 Degree temperatures our guide insisted that we wear wet suits, "The air is warm but those water temperatures are near freezing. If anyone falls in, those wet suits might save your life."

We took his advice and enjoyed a long ride on the swift flowing Alagash River. We ended our run in a quiet, slow moving pool. Now the wet suits became sweltering hot, like wearing long underwear in the Sahara. All of us, including our guide peeled off the tortuous suits and jumped into the frigid water. I jumped but my bathing suit got hung up on the raft air intake valve. I was stuck with my bathing suit hung on the valve like a pair of pants on a line. My bottom was hung on the raft while my feet and head were pinned underwater. I couldn't raise my head to take a breath or kick free of the constriction to swim away. I was helpless. I kept kicking and trying to raise my head but couldn't. "Am I going to die like this?" I wondered. My heart pumping, my lungs desperate for air, I gave one final kick and somehow my suit ripped free. I swam around with the others enjoying the cooling water and my return to life.

I climbed back aboard the raft and was greeted by my friend Peter. He asked, "Charlie, are you okay? I didn't jump in with everybody else but stayed on the raft. I saw you kicking in this weird way and ran over and ripped your suit off. You swam away. Are you okay?"

"Yes Peter, I'm fine but I was in big trouble. I couldn't breathe or swim free. You saved my life. You ripped off my suit or I would've drowned. You saved my life."

That was all that was ever said of the incident. Neither of us ever talked about it again nor brought up the subject on the eight-hour drive back to Cape Cod. It was a strange reaction to a near death situation.

Years later I confronted death again when doctors told me that I had a rare, aggressive type of prostate cancer and that it had metalized into my lungs. They gave me a year to a year and a half to live. I needed surgery, months of chemo-therapy, and later to be put on female hormones. When the Doc suggested the female hormones, I suggested, "Why don't you just chop them off? You can do that here can't you?"

He did the orchiectomy so then I had no balls, no hair, no prostate and a body ballooning from steroids.

That was seven years ago. My point is that I almost lost my life rafting in the Alagash, on Hilton Head confronting cancer and then my sexuality from a doctor's scalpel. Through those challenges I experienced none of the terror that I had during the fifteen panicky minutes of reckless speeding to retrieve my wallet at McDonalds.

Do I really value my wallet more than my life or my gonads?

19
Reflections on Nauset

I sit on Nauset Beach, the sand not only in my shoes but up my bathing suit, all over my torso, in my hair. That's the way I like it. I love Nauset and it has tugged at my heart for forty years. Marilyn and I discovered this place after spending two years in the Army then three more working with another dentist in the Upstate New York village of Cobleskill. It was fine but never felt permanent to either of us so we searched up and down the East Coast, trying to find that special place. As soon as we discovered Nauset, in Orleans on Cape Cod, we knew our search had ended. This is where Marilyn and I laughed, picnicked, sat and watched our kids and ourselves grow up. Her grave is only minutes away. I am happily remarried, moved south to Hilton Head, but Nauset remains "My home." The waves, the sand, the calling of the sea gulls are unlike any other place for me.

Dads still build sand castles with their kids like we did. Rob and Heather were doing that what seems now like yesterday. Here they first ran toward, and then scampered away from the freezing waters. Later they learned to ride those waves and then shouted things like, "Dad did you see that one? It almost got me but I rode it all the way to shore."

I had to catch my breath from My own excitement and exhilaration before responding, "Yes you did. Good job. I had a pretty good ride myself."

"Come on Dad. Here comes another big one. Let's go."

Now I sit in this happy place with the adult Rob and Heather watching other families with children repeat the timeless ritual. They too run in and out of the waves, try to catch the biggest for a body surf to the beach, and then run back for more. I feel the salt and sand in my gray hair and feel at one with these young families.

20
Failure of Osmosis

Osmosis is roughly defined as the pass of a liquid through a membrane, or Absorption by contact.

I spent my fantastic summer of 1958 on Martha's Vineyard as a busboy at the Harbor View Hotel. The boy's dorm was very close to Emily Post elegant summer home. Ms. Post was a snooty newspaper columnist at that time who advised her readers on proper etiquette. She pontificated to anyone who would listen: which fork to use when, which crystal to set out for each wine, and where place cards should be at each table setting. She must have made a lot of money intruding on other people's lives because she lived in a fancy summer house on this magical island.

I was an impressionable seventeen-year-old busboy, escaping parental authority during the summer recess before my senior year in high school. The rest of the staff was made up of, to me, sophisticated college students. They were my models, not Emily. I was their tag-along kid brother, eager to learn from them.

This was my first "serious," summer job. I had to learn from the hotel staff how to set a table, "Forks to the left of the plate, knife to the right and spoons beyond the knife. Folded napkin under the fork. Clear from the right. Serve to the left."

When I came home to Rochester at the end of that fantastical summer, I felt self-satisfied, like a man of the world. Reluctantly, I resumed my inferior position as the youngest at the family dinner table. I regressed to "normal," completion for food. "Grab it or someone else will. Don't stop eating when you're stuffed. Keep pushing it in until you're sick or hate yourself." I transited easily from the staff troth at the Harbor View Hotel to our family competition for bread.

My oldest sister watched the action and asked about my Vineyard neighbor, Emily Post. I'm sure she hoped that some of Emily's class would have rubbed off on me. She was disappointed. I explained that I didn't knowingly see Miss Post all summer but passed her house each day on the way to the beach. Betty warned, "Charles, that was your best chance to gain some manners. You blew it. You're more animalistic now than ever."

I defended myself, "You can't pick up behavior patterns by osmosis. I don't remember seeing her all summer. I passed her house every day but living next to that old fuddy-duddy had no effect on me."

"That's for sure," said Betty

"I watch birds, fish, all those safari animals on TV competing for food and somehow their behavior seems more natural than trying to copy a snobby old lady."

Twenty plus years later, when I was widowed and dating as a "pseudo-mature" adult, my teenage daughter offered some dating tips, "Dad, if you really like a woman, don't take her to a restaurant. Your table manners are atrocious."

I wondered, "Where's Emily? Maybe I should've gotten closer to that old bitch's house. I could've rubbed my head against her wall. Osmosis."

I'm now seventy-six years old and still waiting for my former neighbor to turn me into a mature, mannerly man.

21

Aladdin and Us

We hear so much recently about "fake news." I not sure what that is but even before kindergarten, I recognized one of the fairytales as "fake." Aladdin and his bottle seemed pretty unbelievable. How could that huge genie fit in that small bottle? It couldn't. I recognized "Fake News," before the term is thrown out so casually today. In this famous fable, Aladdin found a magic lamp and when he rubbed it a huge genie sprang out and granted Aladdin three wishes as a reward for freeing him from the bottle. Fables are often told to teach us a lesson and if we can overlook the "fake news," aspect, I think we can learn from this one.

Maybe the magic of the Genie and Aladdin really is inside each one of us. Instead of looking for outside help, the genie, is the secret of achieving our wishes inside each of us? If it is, we're not limited to three wishes, the possibilities of getting what we wish are endless. By changing our attitude and thinking of our desires in a more positive manner, our wishes have a better chance to be granted.

We all speak to ourselves We have internal thoughts and how we think or speak to ourselves can determine if we get our wishes. In the book, "The Secret," this is described as "The Law of Attraction." When we mull over positive thoughts like "I can do it," "I will get it," "I will accomplish my goal," the law of attraction tells us we raise our chances of attaining a positive result. Conversely, if we say, "I can't," "I won't etc. the result will be negative. We won't get what we want.

I'll give an example. In my English as a Second Language class a student from Lithuania and another one from Columbia, South America, both said they read the book The Secret, one in Spanish, the other in Lithuanian. I suggested that the next class we try to read parts of the book in English. So, we read very slowly short passages about the Law of Attraction and how our thoughts and words can determine the result. We had a good discussion and they all seemed to understand the concepts.

When the girl from Columbia struggled through reading some very difficult words to pronounce like "thoughts" and "thorough," she blurted out, "I can't pronounce these words. I'll never learn English. It's hopeless." We all laughed including her at that negative statement and the Lithuanian lady said, "See if you think you can't, you can't. (In this case learn English) With a negative attitude you never will accomplish your goal."

Instead of wasting time looking for our own "Genie," or some other external magic that will bring joy back into our lives. We need to look inside, where our thoughts and wishes would come from. With practice and resolve, learn to control our attitude. By turning off the negativity and turning on the, "I can, I will," button, we have a great chance of success. Your Genie is you. If our internal language is, "I can't,' or, "I won't" there is little chance of getting what we wish for.

I would like to do what the Bible and the field of psychology recommend but it is a challenge. To "Love everybody." is certainly a noble goal and a guarantee of good mental health but if I think it is unachievable, it is. If I walk into a room, look around, and think negatively about a person, "I need to avoid him, he's boring," I will certainly lose in my quest to love him. Maybe I need to remember to not rely on magic or the genie in the bottle, the secret is controlling my internal thoughts. "He's not boring, he's my brother," and reach out to him.

22
A Thief's Revenge

Once, when no one was looking, I grabbed a pint bottle of Smirnoff vodka, two pints of gin, and one Peppermint Snaps. I stuffed them into my jacket and walked from the liquor store into the darkness of the tiny upstate village. I raced to our car, opened the trunk, and threw the loot under our luggage. I sat in the back seat, feeling proud of my bravado, and waited for Frank and Don. They had been distracting the liquor store owner by buying a few bottles of cheap wine while I pocketed the stolen booze.

I looked out the window, but instead of Don and Frank, I stared at the working end of a huge rifle butt. The angry, red faced store owner pointed the rifle at my face and bellowed "Get out of that car kid. I saw you steal from me. Now I'm gonna whip your ass. My neighbor's comin to watch your two buddies, but you're mine." His hair seemed to explode from his head like a caged lion.

I got out of the car, hands up, pleading in a squeeky tone like the girls in my high school classes, "What do you mean. I didn't steal anything. What do you mean?"

"Shut up you little shit. I saw you steal those bottles. Now empty your pockets."

I stood alongside the car, my heart pounding, and turned my pockets inside out. "See. See, they're empty. I don't know what you're talking about."

Don and Frank were now marching towards us with their hands in the air, followed by another townsman brandishing his rifle. "Here Jeb, here's those other two, but are you sure? They showed me their receipt. Here's the two bottles of wine, paid for."

"Hey, what's this all about?" asked my friend Frank. "We're just passin' through this town. Bought a little wine and now you guys are threatening us with guns."

"Ferd, I know these guys stole from me. I saw them do it. They're from the city. I hate city punks. I'm gonna beat this guy to death. You two assholes can watch."

Ferd spoke up. "Jeb, I know you hate city kids. Ever since you got beat by those punks. I don't blame you but these guys had nothin' to do with that." he paused, "Where's their stash? These two showed me their receipt."

Jeb lowered his rifle. It now pointed towards my privates instead of my face, "Turn around you little shit. Show me your back pockets. I know you're a thief."

My back pockets were empty. Ferd asked, "Jeb, are you sure that guy took something? He looks too young to be stealin' and boozin'. Are you sure?"

Jeb had a dreamy, faraway look. He lowered his rifle and listened while Ferd tried to reason with him. "Jeb, you and I have been friends forever. That's why I came runnin' when you called but remember what happened last time with those city kids. You wound up in the pokey for two years. If it happens again they'll throw away the key. Are you sure, Buddy?"

Jeb thought some more, spat on the ground, and took a step towards me. His nose touched mine. His stench sickened me, but I was too frightened to move away, "Look here Punk. I know you stole somethin'. You need a good woppin', but you're not worth the trouble. I hate city assholes but hate prison worse." He took a step back. "Now the three of you get in that car and if I ever see any of you in this town again, you will not get out alive." He poked me in the stomach with the end of his rifle for emphasis, "You, don't even think of comin' this way again."

Don and I took our seats as Frank slipped in behind the wheel of the Chevy and gunned the motor. I started breathing again and yelled, "We are so lucky. If those hicks had looked in the trunk we'd all be dead."

Six years later, I had just graduated from law school and was assigned to assist the public defender in a murder trial against a Mr. Jebson Jenkins. He was accused of beating to death a teenage boy who was passing through that same small town. A crucial piece of evidence that may have showed "Probable Cause," turned up missing during his trial. He is now serving a life sentence for first degree murder and I haven't stolen a thing since that night, years ago.

23
North South

Lorrie and I moved south twenty years ago. Most people would object to Hilton Head, South Carolina as representing true southern culture but the warm air, snowless winters, compensated for the steamy hot, humid summers. A friend welcomed us with this advice, "You know it's summer when you get the morning newspaper and the sweat drips off your shirt before you reenter the house." I loved Cape Cod but would trade of northern winters for summer's heat anytime.

Southerners do live on Hilton Head but it seems like most white people are from Ohio, Michigan, New England, or Indiana,

Southern culture includes so much it is hard to define. It certainly is cooking, accented speaking, maybe a bit of resentment about this "Second Northern Invasion." The first invasion ended, somewhat, at the end of the Civil War. For too many Northerners, Southern culture begins and ends with racism. You don't have to move south to know that that is a horrendous misconception.

I spent the first eighteen years of my life in liberal city of Rochester, New York.

That is the same Rochester that housed Frederick Douglas and from where he wrote his anti-slave, abolitionist newspaper, "The LIberator." His huge statue stands prominently in the middle of Highland Park. Rochestarians take pride in being one of the last stops in the underground railroad, before true freedom rang for escaped slaves in Canada.

The two newspapers, morning and evening were mostly Democratic. They did "like Ike," however over Truman who had the audacity to fire the brave soldier of the Pacific War, General Douglas MacArthur. Northern liberals found comfort in thinking that real racial problems were isolated in the southern states. They pointed out the "down there they" had laws upholding segregation in schools, sidewalks, churches toilets, drinking fountains.

"How awful, it must be down there."

It was indeed awful but it was equally segregated up North. I didn't go to school with a Black person until high school. McKinley Lofton was the only black in a school of 2,000 students. He was looked on in wonder, "Who is he? Why is he here in Monroe High? He 'should be' in Franklin or Madison." I was naive about northern hypocrisy.

My real lesson came one summer when I was a busboy on Nantucket Island. All the hotel /restaurant staff were college students, "Working their way through college," and doing a lot of playing. It was great. Most of the students (staff) were from elite northern schools like Yale, Brown, Boston College, etc. but this was also my first close encounter with fellow human beings from the South.

I was fascinated by a chambermaid, Martha Ann. She had been a homecoming queen at "Ole Miss." I'd pass by the hotel room where she was making beds and cleaning toilets. She'd say in the most melodious way, "Goood moanin' Chuuuck. How'r eyuooo, doin' this moanin'?" I would absolutely melt. That was my first and most wonderful exposure to Southern Charm. It was indeed charming and I was smitten

Also there were "Frog," from Ole Miss and many students from Alabama U. I was also in love with Mary Jo from Florida State. Was that, is that Southern? Anyway, she only had eyes for "Frog," not Charlie.

24

Family Foundations

Grampa McOuat immigrated from Scotland in 1912. He was short, slightly over five feet tall, with a well trimmed mustache and one leg shorter than the other. He wore a built up shoe on one foot but it never evened out his limp. His shoes squeaked so I always knew he was approaching. He settled near other relatives in Rochester, New York and worked as a janitor in a church. As a true Scot, he wa s able to save enough money in a year to send for his wife, Mary Jamison McOuat, his oldest, my father William, who was eight years old, and two younger daughters, my Aunts Jean and Mabel.

As the family patriarch, he did most of the talking at our frequent family "get togethers." He was as loquacious as my father was silent. He led the singing around the piano to Scottish favorites like "Roamin in the Glomen, Just a Wee Dookin' Doris," and every Christian hymn known to man.

I recall one dinner conversation after he returned from a trip to Washington, DC. He said, "The city, the monuments, the museums were wonderful but right next to them was such poverty, such squallor. No one ever talks about that." He did. He sat at the head of a long dinning room table, and lectured, listened a little, and held everyone's attention. One of his favorite topics was the Bible and urged us to do as it said. He emphasized that we "love one another, turn the other cheek, whatever you do to the least of me, that's what you do to me, and lessons like 'The Good Samaritan.'"

He died when I was eight so I never had the opportunity to get to know him as an adult. I remember vividly crying, bawling at his funeral and afterwards being teased by older, wiser cousins because of my public display of grief.

Much later, I was married with children, had a busy dental practice on Cape Cod. An older man came into my office and asked if I was Bill McOuat's son. I proudly said, "Yes, I am."

The man spoke with a heavy, almost unintelligable Scottish accent. He said, "I knew your grandfather very well. I was a banker in Rocherster." He joked, "I hated to see your grandfather come into the bank. He'd go on and on about the great income and wealth inequality in the United States. He assumed we were all rich bankers. When he left my banking cohorts would accuse me of hanging around with communists. Your grandfather was a little guy with a very big heart. He only had a fourth grade education but he read Shakespear, studied history, literature, especially Bobby Burns, and the Bible."

I'm sorry he died before was able to fully understand his diatribes. His son, my father, was the inheriter of values of this little old guy who couldn't ignore poverty in this land of wealth. My own father taught more by example than his garruous father. He was the bread winner, leader of our family, strong and unemotional. This was way before woman's rights became an issue so he was the unopposed leader of the family. He sat at the head of the table with me, his only son seated beside, being made ready to take over this masculine leadership role if anything happened to Papa. My Mother and sisters took their seats at the sides or at the "foot of the table."

One memorable dinner conversation was when my sister came home from high school and stated, "Those Jews all cheat on the exams. I see them copying each other. They're all a bunch of cheaters."

My father in a soft but powerful tone responded, "Flora don't talk that way at this table. It is not only Jews who cheat. They dont cheat anymore than anyone else. It is wrong, wrong to generalize like that." As a young follower of my male role model, I absorbed those words like the mashed potatoes I was injesting.

An earlier incident I will never forget was our family excursion to Charlotte Beach on Lake Ontario. It took two bus transfers and a lot of parental discipline for me to sit in my seat before finally reaching the beach. By the time my pokey father had changed his clothes, ordered me to the toilet, and led the way to the beach my sisters were already spashing around, squealling and laughing with each other in the huge waves.

"Not too far Charles. It's deep out there. Stay in here with me." I did.

I watched my sisters Mary and Flora lying on their life rings, paddling about like queens. I was standing in the shallows, envying my sisters "way out there," when two huge Afro-American boys came running past. They stopped at Flora's life ring and admired the way she could float on the waves, kick her feet and go where ever she wanted. They stood by in wonder.

My father saw their envy, walked out and asked one of them, "Would you like to try it?"

The shortest one's eyes lit up, "Yeah! Can I? Can I?"

Flora hopped off, stood back in horror while one of the Negro boys hopped on her precious ring. I dont think she, I know I, had never seen an Afro-American before. The young boy kicked around for a few minutes, jumped off and thanked my father, then joined his friend out in the deeper water.

Flora now looked at the ring with disdain. "Daddy, I don't want that ring any more. He got his black goo all over it. I don't want it."

My father held the ring, "Come on Flora. THEY ARE JUST LIKE YOU AND ME. THEIR SKIN IS DARKER, THAT'S ALL. Come on. Thanks for being such a big girl and sharing your ring." Flora thought for a minute, hopped back on and probably forgot the incident. I haven't. My first encounter with an Afro-American left his words deeply imbedded within, "THEY'RE JUST LIKE YOU AND ME. THEIR SKIN IS DARKER, THAT'S ALL."

Sixty plus years later when I hear a black, a Jew, a Muslem an Asia, a Latino, etc, etc being denigraded, mistreaated, I take it personally. I get deeply sad and angry.

Did I inherit that trait or was I taught?

25

Two Ghanas

I have volunteered in Ghana many times. I teach at an orphanage school in the capitol city of Accra and in Biakpa, a small isolated village in the mountains.

I remember reading a study that tried to show that as a county's standard of living increases, their "Happiness" inceases. This "study" showed that people in wealthier countries are "happier" than people in poorer countries. The exception was Ghana. At that time, Ghana wasn't wealthy but rated highly on this study's happiness scale.

I have indeed found Ghanains unusually friendly, family oriented, welcoming, and with pride in their country and culture. That patriotic pride and joy may have reached its peek during one of my visits. The newly elected President of the United States, Barack Obama, chose Ghana as the first African country that he would officially visit as our president. I was lucky enough to witness their joy, pride, and enthusiam for their country and support of our president. American flags flew everywhere. A common chant was "Ghana, Ghana, President Obama, the United States" I too felt pride in my country and thankful for my good luck in being there during his visit.

I smiled as I watched their clapping, singing, and dancing in enthusiastic welcome. Ghanains who couldn't participate in the parades were glued to their TVs watching every minute of the pagentry and glamour. He addressed their Parliament in a frank, respectful tone. His plea for them was, "If you want to attract American investment you need to clean up corruption in government and business." Wow ! My initial reaction was that he was talking down to them, lecturing about what "they should be doing." They were not insulted. Only an Afro-American like Barack Obama could get away with such frankness with the Africans.

Despite his honesty with them, their enthusiasm for our president and nation continued, with red, white, and blue flags flying everywhere. It was still early in my stay when I heard Air Force One fly overhead carrying President Obama back home and leaving Ghanains with puffed out chests and an exuberant love of the United States. That was early in his presidency and reflected the first of two Ghanas that I have experienced.

The second Ghana is evolving today. When they hear our forty fifth president labelling Haiti and other countries as "Shit Hole Countries," they ask me, "What is going on? What's happening? I'm scared."

I can give no explanation, no reassurance. I can only respomd that I am deeply ashamed, scared like them, and not proud of our leader in The White House.

Then they ask about the almost weekly slaughter of innocent children in our schools. "Is that really happening? What is going on? Why can't something be done?" Why, indeed. I could try to describe the NRA, Hollywood violence, dysfunctional families, mental health, drugs, political incompetence, etc.

It's frustrating, scary, and very sad but I can give no explanation to my Ghanain friends nor to anyone else.

26

Two Poets and a Piker

I have always been baffled by poetry. I have taken poetry appreciation classes, even a poetry writing class. Poetry is the adumbration of an intellectual. It is the most concise form of writng, full of symbols, rhythm, and often hidden meanings that will forever be hidden from me. In my younger days I could understand some *New Yorker* cartoons but never once have I understood one of their poems. If being published in the *New Yorker* is the gold standard of what is good or trite poetry, why are their poems so unintelligible to any but the few?

I didn't realize until taking poetry classes in Life Long Learning on Hilton Head that I have had contact with some elite poets. Last year we were reading a poem by the acclaimed Marge Piercy. She has published nineteen books of her own poetry, and is held in highest esteem by her literary colleges. When our class was discussing her work, I raised my hand. while suppressing a laugh, I said, "I knew Marge Piercy. She was a patient in my Cape Cod dental office. She was always reading or writing, sometimes even while being treated. I almost considered her a friend until one Saturday, she called my emergency number and requested that I clean her teeth that day. I answered, "No, I only treat emergencies on Saturday." She hung up and on Monday called my office to have her records sent to another office. That was the end of my "relationship" with poet Marge Piercy.

This year in our class we started with Robert Frost and worked our way through several poet lauriates and other famous poets. We came to something written by Wilderness Sarchild. This time I was unable to control my excitement at the recognition of an old Cape Cod acquaintance. "Wilderness Sarchild?" I shouted, disturbing the seriousness of the class,. "I knew her. We used to run together. Six o'lock in the morning. I ran with a bunch of guys. One morning this very long haired Peggy Escher intruded on our male bonding. She was a feminist before it became popular.

One day she announced to all the guys. "Ray and I are getting a divorce. I am no longer Peggy Escher. From now on my name is Wilderness Sarchild."

After pushing ourselves through another torturous sunrise jog, my friend Jim asked, "Peggy… err ah… no.. What is it 'Wilderness?' How did you choose that name?

She said, "I like being in the forrest, the wildernes. I am no longer Ray's wife. My mother's name is Sara. Therefore I choose to be called, 'Wilderness Sarchild.'"

I sort of giggled on the drive home, "Wilderness Sarchild?" How wierd is that?

Months later, she introduced us to the new man in her life, a short, bearded, hippie looking guy, with thick glasses named Chuck.

I think she soon tired of the morning self torure and went on with her life. Now, probably forty years later, in this year's class I was shocked to learn that long haired, 'Wilderness' and her hippie boy friend Chuck are now a well publicized, highly esteemed poets.

I am proud to have known Marge Piecy and Wilderness. I even stuck my fingers in Marge's mouth and greeted the rising Cape Cod sun with Wilderness. They are famous while I remain undiscovered. I have self published three books and will soon come out with a fourth. I enjoy writing but have had limited financial success. How limited? On June 28, 2018 I received a royalty check of $ 1.26, with withholding of .49. That may be the definition of "limited financial success."

27

Voodoo

Voodoo has gotten a sometimes well deserved, "bad name." I remember childhood black and white movies where an evil looking villian put a spell on an innocent beauty. He sucked her blood, she swooned, keeled over and died in agony.

I was witness to its slightly more subtle power when I first visited Haiti. Haiti is the poorest country in the western hemisphere and among the poorest in the world. I first went there in 1983 and had never seen such poverty. People wore rags, with bones protruding from their starving, skeletal bodies, sleeping in tin or cardboard shacks. Any employment able to sustain food, clothing, and shelter was limited to supporters of "the Man" in power. The despot of that time was Baby Doc Duvalier who inherited his lofty position from his corrupt father Papa Doc. They both controlled their fellow Haitians by intimidation with their Tonton Maccou henchmen and manipulation by voodoo.

Voodoo was, and is, an attempt by believers to form some relationship with their gods and give some explanation for human suffering. Papa Doc manipulated his people by warning that if they didn't support him, he could put curse on them, causing illness, death and life long misery. His son continued those diabolical policies for years. It was sad for me to witness this "otherworldly power," used by these depots to control the desperate Haitians.

I experienced some positive aspects of voodoo in Ghana. My host, mentor and guide was a proud African named Tony. He wanted to expose me to every aspect of his culture during my stay in his village. For examplle, one morning on the way to the school, we stopped by the wayside to sample some palm wine with the village elders as they sacrificed a chicken over burning embers.

Another day I was ushered into a small building that was housing the embalmed corpse ot the "paramount chief" who had died two years before. The four corners of the coffin were guarded by fiece looking warriors, armed with curved sabers. They looked straight ahead, not at me as I respectfully passed by the departed chief.

One morning he asked, "Would you like to visit the voodoo man?"

"Yes. Of couse. Let's go."

We drove for hours over clay, muddy roads and non roads until stopping at a small compound. He introduced me to a heavy set man, maybe fifty years old wearing a t-shirt, shorts and sandals. He was sitting in a plastic easy chair in the middle of the compound. Surrounding us were four typical African houses. Tony pointed out one that was where tthe voodoo man stayed with his wife. His family lived next to him and the third house was his "office," or where he saw patients. The fourth house was empty of live human beings. I was reserved for departed ancestors and living spirits. I sat in my own plastic chair facing the voodoo man and Tony sat off to the side.

The voodoo man said that he had had a career as a school administrator but also had been a voodoo man through all of his adult years. His father was a voodoo man before him. He explained the similarities to our Christian religion. "We also have a supreme god who has helpers, like your angels."

I asked about the healing power of voodoo. "Oh yes. I use herbs, chants, like your prayers, songs, like your hymns."

I leaned forward. I didn't want to miss a word. "Do you ever work together with the conventional health care system?"

"Oh yes. I often refer cases to them and they refer cases to me. For example, I treated my wife for her for high blood pressure but when her pressure remained high, I referred her to her to a medical doctor. He prescribed medicine and her blood pressure is now normal."

"One example out of the many cases that they refer to me may be marrital tensions" I discussed that with him and felt like I was talking with a psychologist in the USA. "I listen to them, then try to get them to talk with each other" etc.

When we take a drug, its effectiveness may be due to the drug itself or simply the placebo effect. If we think it will be helpful it will be. How different is that from the Ghanain voodoo man?

I have been taking local bee polin for my allergies. It seems to help. Who cares if it's due to the placebo effect or the polin as long as symtoms improve. I think tomorrow I'll start on apple-cider vinegar. My sister tells me that it helps with her arthritis. Why not give it a try? Any other suggestionns?

28
What's in a Name?

Charles John McOuat is my name. Charles is from my Mother's father, who died before my birth. John and McOuat are from my father's Papa. The McOuats were Scottish immigrants. I couldn't understand them when they talked and that may have started my life of confusion.

My father was a piper, my sisters danced the Highland Fling. I resisted. I didn't want to be seen wearing a skirt, a kilt. I bought my first kilt three years ago. I would now wear it proudly but there are few suitable occasions.

Charles comes from my mother's father. They were farmers. My mother escaped the farm drudgery by coming to Rochester, NY, where she dated my Father for 7 years before they got married. They had to save enough money to buy a house before tying the knot. They had three girls before me. I was the only boy, the youngest, and was doted upon by all the family females.

Maybe that is why today, I expect all women to treat me like a cute, loveable. little boy. I, Charlie, am 76 years old and now suspect that those expectations from women may be the cause of some of the difficulties I've had in my relationship with the opposite sex. Who Me???

POETRY

1

The Dead of Winter

When trees shed their leaves, turn brown, fall to the ground
Days short and frigid, nights long and dark, called,
"The Dead of Winter." Symbolizing death to some.
But also a sure sign of Spring,
With buds on the trees, blossoms on bushes
A new life, an awakening, our world reborn, It's Spring.

When aches, pains, and forgetfulness become an accepted part of life,
And you can't remember if you've taken your pill yet today
That too can be seen as a foreshadowing of death, "The Dead of Winter."
It can also be a wakeup call, a heralding,
Get moving, learn, teach, travel, read a new book, reread an old one, mentor a child
"Jump into Spring, feel a new life within, be reborn, like Spring."

When I see eight-year-old Sara in Ghana, hand in the air, desperate to learn
She may have to drop out of school, parents can't afford $35 per year fees
I do nothing, the "Dead of Winter fills my soul"
When I help Sara, hear the excitement in her voice when she calls me "Uncle Charlie,"
"I jump into Spring, feel a new life within, am reborn, like Spring."

James in Haiti, taught himself English, 30 words per day, he says,
Sleeps in an 8 by 8 cement block hovel, on a dirt floor,
A soiled rug over him and his mother. I do nothing,
Afraid I'll build dependency, "The Dead of Winter fills my soul."
When I help him, then see him help other Haitians who have even less than he does,
"I jump into Spring, feel a new life within, am reborn, like Spring."

In ESL class, a room full of motivated students, a daunting task
I wonder, "Twenty years of doing this, too much, too long?"
Someone else's turn? "The Dead of Winter fills my soul."
I help them with their new language, they help their children with their schoolwork,
See them get a better job, better able to contribute to our community.
"I jump into Spring, feel a new life within, am reborn, like Spring."

I visit Sandalwood, the Corridor of Shame
My neighbors, friends, family, a stranger, people in this room, I know they are struggling
I do nothing, It's none of my business. "The Dead of Winter fills my soul,"
I reach out, care, hug, listen without giving advice.
I realize we're all brothers, sisters,
"I jump into Spring, feel a new life within, am reborn, like Spring."

2
Maybe

I want to go to Ghana
    To see some African friends
I have to see these people
    Before my good life ends
To joke and speak with the students
    At Foster Orphanage School
And walk the streets in sandals
    Oh, that would be so cool.
What's happened to Victoria and Sara
    And others? Forgot their names.
I taught them math and science
    And played their African games.
Remembering Mary, "Like mother of Jesus,"
    Narrows time and space between us.
We laughed, sang songs, jumped rope
    I breathe and dream, have hope.
Biakpa, Accra, Hue, and Ho
    To return I ask, "No mo', No mo'.

3
Cleaning Day

Sniff, cough, choke; Woke this morning like I'm gonna croak
Mopey, third week of this, must do something.
Clean out an old desk, mold, mildew that's the culprit
Scrape, scrub, scour delve into hidden crevices.
Wow, What's that? One hundred forty dollars in bills
Two fifties, two twenties, cash forgotten.
Feeling better, Hmm, cured my ills
And here, silver dollars 1922, 23, 1925.
Where'd they come from? Who knows?
Two, four, six in all, a Yippee surprise.
Congested? Sick? Coughing no more.
A philatelist, he'll make me rich.
Zippity do dah, Zip, Zip, Zip
Turned my "Achoo," I'm sick day, into "Zowie" I'm cured day.
But, would if this silver brings no wealth?
Does treasure control my mind, my health?
Guess I have the same weakness as many
Think too much 'bout money, money, money.
Hope not. Feelin' just fine
Touch my toes, make a rhyme

The value of this silver, Wait and see
It's the lesson learned that set me free.
"A dose of optimism,
An injection of positive thoughts
Cured my headache, runny nose, my cough."
If so, how about cancer? Heart disease? The mopes?
And that nagging list of dashed hopes?
A panacea! Eureka! Yes, Yes, Yes
Hurrah, Halleluiah, Zip, Yip, YYYYep

4

Greatest Failure

A steady progression from hunter- gatherers to agriculture
To industry, now technology
From family to group to tribe to state to nation
All to protect, be inclusive, progress, move upwards
Our brains become more complex, more trained, educated
    Is it working????

But why have we made so little progress, surely regressed
With our biggest challenge Racism, Bigotry, Prejudice.
Looking down on someone who's different
Our habit, our humanity, could it be our demise?
We use our brains to build bigger, better, more efficient.
Our superior brain, this superior organ has failed to show us how…
To respect, be a good neighbor, see the positive in a person.
Are we forever going to be hampered, limited by our prejudice?
Can't we rise above looking at a different skin color,
Eye structure, accent, upbringing and judging:
He's Black so he's this… She's Latino so she's that…
They're Asian so they…. They're Indian so he….
Racism, Bigotry, Prejudice keeps us
Angry, Stressed, Hating, Unhealthy, Stuck in quicksand.
We need something more powerful than neurons and synapse
Help, We're Failing, Falling, Desperate, Dying.

5

A Knock at the Door

Christmas lights brighten the house
A dark, frigid night, cozy inside
A knock at the door
The police chief, my friend Chet
Could only mumble, "Call this number."
His manner, I stiffened, *What's wrong? What's happening?*
I dialed, "I'm Dr. Jones. I'm sorry,
Your wife. Killed in a car accident.
She never made it to the hospital."
I screamed, "Did some drunk hit her?"
Don't remember his answer.
Only now Chet managed a whisper,
"She was hit by a senile driver, wrong side of the highway. Head on."
Don't remember the details. Only telling my twelve-year-old son,
"Rob, Your Mom. She won't be home,
She died, a car accident."
We screamed, we hugged, we cried such tears.
Then his sister, ten years old, came downstairs,
Her hair wrapped in a wet towel, a white bathrobe
A frightened look, "Heather, I'm sorry. Mom. A car accident,

She's dead," Shocked, startled. silent.
Heather, the emotional one, her Mom, her best friend,
She couldn't cry, No words. *Not true, can't be. Not Mom. Not my Mommy.*
Then more knocks, Friends, Townspeople,
More hugs, tears, screaming, yelling
Five hours later the stream of mourners unabated.

My wife, my love, mother of our two, gone, kids with no Mom
Sleepless, I hear cars driving by all night
They wonder, "What will they do?"
I ponder, tossing in an empty bed, "What will we do?"
What will I do? What will we do?" Marilyn gone.

6

Lee Shore

Alas, to the sailor, long at sea
The lee shore is home, the hearth with hot tea.
Trading his hammock for feather bed
The familiar, fido, friends, family.
It's safety, protection, a goal well achieved.
Hard days behind, now solid ground.

Ah, but Lad, beware the lee shore
It's rocks and wrecks, disasters galore
With drownings and dangers, death even more.
Dichotomous symbols, this lee shore
Contentment, a goal achieved, one strived for
Or to be avoided, danger, disaster.
The wise sailor must choose
Sail on, or turn to, head out to sea.

Ah, the sea, sunrise, sunset book endings each day,
Whales spouting, starlit skies, dolphins at play.
A safe harbor, seductive, but too much comfort
Yields boredom. A stagnant life is no life.
Turn to Lad. Ships are built to survive heavy seas
Not to rot where it's safe. Turn to Lad, windward you'll be.

Recalling my own seventy-five years
My greatest accomplishments from casting off from comfort
Heading into the wind, away from the lee.
Cobleskill in the Catskills, financial security
Perfect for four of us to grow together
A small college town. But me? I was restless.
To have my own practice to live by the sea.
Knowing nothing of business or what laid ahead
We moved to Orleans, Cape Cod. Oh, my what a dream.
But could I pay bills? Did I make a bad choice?
Things got better, much better in fact. That decision, our best
The Cape with its treasures, the people, the rest.

Other choices I've made, just like that
Some worked out, some didn't, regretting none.
Restlessness, a sign "get moving," it says,
Flee from stagnation, boredom, long days,
Push on you might, from the Lee of Life
Make a choice, the lee friend or foe?
A peaceful place or a world of woe?

7
Writing Poetry

Writing poetry is easy, at least for me,
    But not right now, have no time free.

The poems I'll write, they'll bring fortune and fame,
    But first I'll call, "Old What's his name?"

For me poetry never, ever bores
    But first must do my household chores

I'm lucky, ideas flow into my head
    But wait, not now, that book needs be read.

I'm determined, this moment, it's going to be great
    But I have an appointment, can't be late

I never procrastinate
    But Audre that poem will have to wait

Poems require a sort of rhythm
    Too many go on Ad Infinitum

As I said before, this writing is easy
    If only I didn't feel so queasy.

I'm never one to let things in the way
    Surely tomorrow, can't do it today.

My friend Audre says, "Give it a try."
    Can't find the time, don't know why.

Her poetry class will be so much fun
    But no time now, I've got to run.

8

A Gym Rat's Lament

Four days a week, I go to the gym
Stretching, lifting, to try and get slim.
Chin ups, pull ups, all I can do
But I look in the mirror, wonder, Who?
Wrinkled, saggy, who's that guy?
He's grown old, I wonder, Why?
T's not booze, late hours, that've done him in,
So, what's the cause of his double chin?
It's eating, eating, he likes to binge.
He'll eat anything that doesn't eat him.
He does quite well 'til eleven thirty
Then look out, he'll wolf a whole turkey.
Apples, nuts, a loaf of bread
What goes wrong inside his head?
No donuts, cake, and no ice cream
But he eats enough for a football team.
What's wrong with Charlie, he'd like to know
That tummy of his continues to grow
No self-control, he needs a shrink
It's Lorrie's fault, don't you think?

9

Dark Hooded Man

Knocking, Knocking, Knocking at My Door
Four days a week I'm at the gym
Treadmill, weights to keep me trim
I push harder every week
A healthy bod' is what I seek
Still the dark hooded man comes knocking, knocking, knocking at my door

Too much stress I cannot take
Meditate, meditate for good health's sake
Multivitamins to start the day
All the docs say that's a good way
Still the dark hooded man comes knocking, knocking, knocking at my door.

Plenty of veggies piled high
Also fruit but not with a pie
I've given up glutens, pasta too
Get all my shots including flu
Still, the dark hooded man comes knocking, knocking, knocking at my door

I have noticed as I get older
Morning and night, I say a prayer
Haven't missed church in more than a year
But the knocking continues, and with it fear
The dark hooded man comes knocking, knocking, knocking at my door

10
Thursday SPRAWL

I love Thursday, the day of SPRAWL
To read and write with y'all.
Ten years it's been for me and Brian
A valued friendship, that ain't lyin.'
Years ago, my scalp was bare
Til' Brian brought me Harpo Hair.

The newest member, Gorgeous Gail
Talented rhymer, a welcomed gal.
Merrill brought us class form Yale
Hilton Head history, an adventurous tale
He has cycled with Moroccan Berbers
Damned if I'll eat a Pasco Burger

Now I'll tell the point of this ditty
The next two weeks, I'll be not with yee.
April twenty, I'm off to Boston
To be with Rob, don't see him often.
Alone we'll be just him and me
No wives or kids, we'll be set free.

The following week, Heather's here
Can't miss a chance to hug, drink beer.
Husband Joe and little Mikey
Laughs galore, highly likely.
Next two weeks, I can't do SPRAWL
But the week after that, back with y'all.

Note; SPRAWL is South Carolina Readers and Writer's League. or
THE GUILD

Printed in the United States
By Bookmasters